Lion at My Heart

Lion at My Heart

A NOVEL BY

HARRY MARK PETRAKIS

An Atlantic Monthly Press Book

Little, Brown and Company

Boston · Toronto

ATLANTIC–LITTLE, BROWN BOOKS
ARE PUBLISHED BY
LITTLE, BROWN AND COMPANY
IN ASSOCIATION WITH
THE ATLANTIC MONTHLY PRESS

*Published simultaneously in Canada
by Little, Brown & Company (Canada) Limited*

PRINTED IN THE UNITED STATES OF AMERICA

To my father and mother,
and the land from
which they came

Lion at My Heart

Chapter 1

THE SNOW BEGAN TO FALL IN THE AFTERNOON. THE flakes were large and swept lazily across the window of Rothstein's Discount Liquor Store, where I stood leaning on the handle of a broom. The snow drifted across the taverns and groceries and coffeehouses on Dart Street. The kids wearing oversized leather jackets and flapping boots were already sliding and screaming upon the walks.

"For half your hourly wage," Rothstein said, and he spoke with his short fat body sitting sprawled across a case of beer, "I could obtain the services of a scholar who would recite the Talmud for me while leaning on a broom. As a barbarian, your function is to sweep, sweep, sweep and make clean the floor."

"I am meditating on the falling snow," I said without

3

moving. "Do you realize at this moment the snow is probably falling all over the city? On the packinghouses and across freights in the yards at Canal Street. On the long girders of the El, and on all the busy Walgreen Drug Stores. On Oak Street and Rush Street and Halsted Street and Comiskey Park. Right here on the pride of the bush, Rothstein's Discount Liquor Store with specials all at attractive prices."

"You are young and a poet," Rothstein said. "All I can see is the sidewalk that must soon be shoveled."

"You are chained to the earth," I said.

"And you are insolent."

The front door opened and Orchowski, the big iron-faced policeman on the beat, came in shaking and stamping off the snow. He was a huge and heavy man and the floor shook under him.

Rothstein waved his hands in mock delight.

"Here is the man who will tell us about the snow," he said. "Tell us, O descendant of Pharaoh and pilferer of stray apples and peaches, what do you see in the snow?"

Orchowski scowled and removed his cap and dusted off the snow.

"A car skidded on Laramie a while ago and hit a post," he said. "One guy was killed and the other guy was mangled. Made a hell of a mess."

"Why am I so lucky," Rothstein said and he beat his chest with his fists. "For a clerk I have a poet who leans on a broom. For a friend a uniformed undertaker with

4

a casualty report to cheer me up. My wife's oldest brother, who sells girdles, should be so lucky."

I put the broom behind the counter and reached for my jacket on the hook.

"It is Thanksgiving," I said. "I am going home. We have turkey and dressing and good Greek wine that was not bought from Rothstein's Discount Liquor Store. The holiday rush is over."

"Who will shovel the walk?" Rothstein asked.

"A little exercise will do you good," Orchowski said.

"It is impolite to speak when you have not been spoken to first," Rothstein said.

"When it stops snowing and if I can still move after dinner," I said, "I will come back and shovel off the snow."

"I do not ask for miracles," Rothstein said. He got up heavily and took a bottle from the shelf and put it in a bag. "You are a Greek and take your eating very serious. After dinner you will collapse. My regards to your father. Give him this fine brandy from me."

"You have a full case of that brandy gathering dust in the back room," I said. "We haven't sold a bottle in a year. My father will be pleased you thought of him."

"Get out, cynic," he said. "Go stick your head in the snow."

I laughed and left the store.

I walked down Dart Street and crossed at the corner. The snow swept around my ears and wet my cheeks. I passed the south gate of the mill and the snow sparkled across the stacks and gabled roofs of the buildings and upon the ore cars waiting at the sidings. The blast furnaces with the heating stoves beside them looked like great snowmen with children clustered around. Most of the furnaces were banked and the rolling mills down for the holiday. There was a strange stillness in the air as if the falling snow had muffled all sound.

Our house was on Carnaba Street about a block from the south gate and almost under the shadow of the slab mill. A house like any of a hundred other houses around the mills, squatting dark and cramped between buildings on either side, with the soot and dust of the mills heavy upon the eaves. I suppose each man thought his house was different and for each man it was true. The exteriors were the same, but my family had lived in our house for twenty-seven years. My ma had died in that house and my brother Mike and I had been born there. That made it different to us.

In our back yard a snowball shot past my ear and a moment later I ducked a second one and spotted Lenny Lanaras poised to throw again. I reached down and packed one of my own and hurled it back, but he had hidden behind a fence and hooted.

I opened the back door into the warm big kitchen, into the delicious scents of roasting turkey and spiced dressing and warm oven-crisp bread. I thought again of Ma dead for so many years. I thought of her mostly

6

when the holidays came around, like this Thanksgiving, with a neighbor woman in to cook our meal and with Pa and Mike and me and maybe old Simonakis sitting at the table to eat.

Mrs. Lanaras, built like a barrel and red-cheeked from cooking, came into the kitchen slipping into her coat.

"One more hour for the bird," she said. "Cranberries in the icebox and *yaurti* in the jar on the sink. Make holler if you need me." She went out the door screaming to round up her kids.

I walked through the dining room and the hall and into the parlor. Pa sat reading the paper in his big chair under the lamp. His presence there gave the room a sense of warmth and order. He heard me and looked up.

"You late," Pa said. "Teacher keep fathead after school?"

"No school today, Pa," I said. "I was at the store. And besides, in college the teachers don't keep you after school. They are glad to let you go early."

"I forget you not have school today," Pa said, and a little smile worked at the corners of his mouth. "I so glad have damn college boy for son, I want you always there."

"When I graduate next year, Pa," I said, "I'll become a famous teacher like Socrates. Everybody will be chasing you and asking for your autograph because you are my old man."

He shook his head dolefully.

"Just try not be kick out," he said. "You got big handicap. You come from family with hardest heads in old country."

I laughed and went over and sat on the side of his chair and he gave my head a shove. I put my arm around his shoulders, feeling them still big and hard under the furnace of years and all the steel he had rolled. Mike always said that Pa's head could have been cut out of steel with the alligator shears. He had the strong proud head of a lion, with iron-gray and close-cropped curly hair above a thick corded neck. The way he looked at me, his eyes and cheeks showing the fierce love he had for me, the pride he took in me, son of his flesh and blood.

"Go take bath," he said, and he gave me another shove that almost tumbled me on the floor. "You stink."

"How can you tell?" I asked. "After all your years in the mill, how can you tell any other stink from your own?"

I ducked the paper he threw at me and went from the room and up the stairs. In the bathroom I started to strip and saw the clean towels hanging on the rack. Mrs. Lanaras must have put them there. I remembered then that Mike was bringing Sheila Cleary home for the first time to meet Pa.

I had never seen this Irish girl my older brother was crazy about. I knew that her parents were dead and she

8

lived outside the bush with her aunt. Mike had met her one night at a dance. They had been seeing each other for five or six weeks, and maybe because he couldn't talk to Pa, he bent my ear. On nights when he came home after being out with her, he would come into my room and wake me and sit on the edge of my bed telling me about his blue-eyed descendant of the grand Kings of Ireland.

"Go to sleep," I said. "For cri' sakes go to sleep or you'll wake Pa."

He laughed and his strong face was more like Pa's than mine and maybe with more of Pa's iron.

"I go for this girl," he said. "Honest, Tony, I can't sleep for thinking about her. I like everything about her. The way she looks, the way she talks. Thinking about her is driving me nuts."

I doubled my pillow and twisted over on my side. I thought forebodingly of Pa and how he felt about Mike and me getting serious about any girl not a Greek.

"Goddammit, I'm in love," Mike said. "You don't know how it feels. You feel good and think crazy. She's got eyes you could lose yourself in, deep and blue, and I feel her inside me like a furnace."

"What about Pa?"

The skin around his mouth got tight.

"He has got to understand. That old country crap is for the birds. If you love a girl, it don't make any difference whether she is damn Greek or not." He paused and looked down for a long moment at his big hands. "Maybe if Ma was still alive she could help make him understand."

Maybe if Ma was still alive. I was seven and Mike twelve when she died. The last year we watched her daily grow more pale and thin, the skin of her cheeks becoming dark and dry, her fingers dark and stiff. I remembered the fat nurse in white, drinking coffee and smoking a cigarette in the kitchen. Mostly I remembered Pa sitting for hours beside Ma's bed holding her hand, neither of them moving for a long time, I was sure, until Mike and I came into the room. My ma would laugh softly and tell us we wore faces like sad old women and send us out to play in the sunshine.

I don't remember how long it took Ma to die but that sometime before my eighth birthday she was dead.

For a while we had a woman to take care of us and she smelled of apple blossom bath salts, and then Pa caught her using a birch rod on Mike's back and threw her out. Mike had played hookey from school, and when Pa found out, he beat him himself. After that, he took care of us. Sometimes he slapped me for not listening, but mostly I remembered how gentle his big hands could be toweling me dry after a bath or helping me dress on a Sunday morning for church. He shined our shoes and cooked our breakfast and made sandwiches for our school lunches. He joined the P.T.A. and attended the meetings, fiercely taking part in programs that were planned, and even learned to sew buttons on our clothes. That was something to see. At night we said our prayers together, and he tucked us into bed. He kissed us good night and the needles of his beard were rough against my cheek and the smell of mill dust was on his clothes. He would stand for a last moment in the doorway, his broad body almost blocking out the light from the hall. I would close my eyes, warm and comforted, because I was in his house.

"I'm going to bring Sheila home for Thanksgiving," Mike said. "I told Pa and he don't like it, but by God, if he wants me at his table, he will have to take her too."

"Sure," I said. "There is nothing wrong with bringing a girl home to dinner."

But I was not sure. Mike had grown up, gone through the war, and was working with Pa in the mills. I was a senior in college. Pa was the way he was, and I marveled at Mike's courage in crossing him. Not because I was afraid of Pa but because I knew how much he loved both of us. Since Ma died, Pa and Mike and I had been as close as a family could be.

When I finished showering and dressing, I went downstairs. Pa was in the kitchen with Spiro Simonakis, who lived across the alley in a desolate furnished room. Simonakis was a bald and bullet-headed Homer who had never married, made few friends, and was now retired from the mills. When Mike and I were younger, he would shoot us into sleep and nightmares with his stories. He remembered the bloody steel strike of 1919 and had a hundred tales to tell of the fire and the fighting and the lines of militia. He would tell us of the heroes and legends of the mills and of the myths of ancient Greece and sometimes he got the blood and thunder all mixed up and the heroes in a snarl. In the end, Achilles tapped an open hearth in Gary and Joe Magarac fought beneath the walls of Troy. But he made them real and alive as living men. Pa swore that Simonakis was the mightiest liar in any mill in the country, but I think he swore mostly at what they had in common. They were both tough with a crust of arrogance covering emotion. Even more indigestible was that Simonakis was the only man in blocks who could give Pa a battle at checkers. They fought over that game like dogs over a bone and hollered and cursed. Sometimes again they played in silence so intense you felt a strand of rubber was being stretched to the breaking point. This might last for hours, until late in the night I would wake from sleep to the sound of a wild bellow and a string of curses. This meant either one or the other had finally won.

Now the two of them had the roasted turkey on a platter on the kitchen table.

"Mrs. Lanaras said one hour," I said, "It hasn't been an hour yet."

Pa looked at me with scorn and pointed to the turkey. "Done," Pa said. "Goddam bird is done. Ten minutes more would make black. Ten minutes more, we begging sausage from Mrs. Lanaras."

"Doesn't look done to me," I said.

He motioned helplessly to Simonakis. "Black day when son goes to college." He waved in the direction of the mills. "Better I send him work at furnaces. Learn tell when turkey done."

"A skill that takes years to acquire," Simonakis said somberly. "It should be a required subject in college."

I went to the icebox and got out the tray of fresh cranberries, dark red with the darker seeds.

"You should both be professors," I said. "One could teach turkey watching and the other could teach checkers."

Pa, who had begun to slice the round crisp-crusted bread, looked at me soberly for a moment and then made a spitting sound through his teeth.

"You so damn smart," he said. "Only part of turkey you get is ass."

"Mercy, Pa," I said. "I'm starved."

"Do not give up hope," Simonakis said. "I will use my influence." He smiled wryly. "In return for the breast of the turkey for you, I will spot him two checkers the next time we play. I am several pieces better than he anyway."

I looked at Pa's face, and he had gotten red and was

just beginning to rumble when there was a knock on the back door. I opened it and Father Kontoyannis stood in the doorway shaking off the snow.

He was the priest of the small Greek Orthodox church of St. Sophia across the river, beside the union hall on Barrows Street. A cleft-jawed man of slight build in his early sixties with a shock of wiry white hair. A mobile face that seemed to change expression swiftly. A voice moving from sardonic humor to gentleness to blunt suggestions on the role of God. He came into the kitchen smiling.

Pa put down the bread knife. "In back door, Father, like grocery boy deliver tomatoes? Why not come front?"

Father Kontoyannis shrugged. "It makes no difference, Angelo, front door or back door. If the house has friends, I will enter by the window." He smiled again and said hello to me and looked at Simonakis.

"You have not been to church in several weeks," he said. "Maybe you are getting personal messages from God?"

Simonakis scowled a little.

"If you are concerned for my dimes," he said, "I will write you out a check."

Father Kontoyannis measured him closely with a slight smile turning the corners of his mouth. "I would frame it," he said. "As evidence that you are a Christian." Pa laughed and Simonakis glared at him. "If I knew you prayed alone, Spiro," the priest went on, "I

14

would not care. I think, however, unless you pray with others you become careless. You would be content in the old pantheon with many Greek gods. But be careful. If I were you, I would not miss church too often. You never know when a Sunday service will be your last."

"You are almost as old as me," Simonakis said. "You be careful too."

The priest winked at me.

"I have already made my reservations," he said. "I will go parlor car and hope only coach passengers go to hell."

Pa laughed again loudly and even Simonakis had to smile. That was the pungent way the priest talked. There was no sugar off his square tongue, and if a man wanted to indulge in only the posturings of worship, he cut his nonsense quick. This offended a number of the shopkeepers who were part of the congregation, and a half dozen times in the past few years there had been petitions started to oust him from his church. He was accused of irreverence and drinking too much and visiting the house of a widow a number of times late at night. Each time the forces came to grips, Pa and the mill men saved him. I was glad because even as a child I could remember the priest so often in our house, eating at our table, sitting on our porch in the late lazy afternoons of summer as the shifts changed and the men walked by on their way home.

The front bell rang. I looked at Pa and could see him suddenly uneasy remembering Mike and the girl.

"I'll get it," I said.

He shook his head and rubbed his hands on a towel.

"We go to door together," he said. He turned to the priest. "My son brings home girl from Irish house. Greek girl is not good enough." He was ashamed before the priest and Simonakis.

"There are worse things than that, Angelo," Father Kontoyannis said.

"When a foreigner enters the house," Simonakis said, "the first step in the destruction of the family begins."

Pa glared at him.

"You are goat!" he said. "Shut big mouth and pour wine for Father."

I started to the front door and he followed me through the house muttering under his breath. I opened the door and Mike stood there with the girl.

I think both Pa and I were taken back because they were covered with snow. They stood there for a moment shaking the flakes off their coats, and she wore some kind of a plaid babushka over her hair. Her eyes were large and clear blue and her brows were slim and delicate crowns. Her mouth was red and full and glistening wetly from the snow. The babushka suddenly reminded me of the weary-faced Greek and Polish women bent with years and the breeding of too many daughters and sons. They wore babushkas in winter and summer to cover the unkempt hair they could perhaps no longer bother to comb or brush. They walked the streets about the mills and wore their weariness like a poorly fitted coat. I felt sorry for them and tried to remember my mother and could not believe she had ever looked like that.

Mike stepped inside and brought Sheila beside him.

"Pa, this is Sheila," Mike said. He spoke with a hard set to his jaw and a glint in his eyes.

"Merry Thanksgiving Day, Mr. Varinakis," Sheila said, and her voice was pleasing and she pronounced our name clearly and correctly as if she had made sure of that.

"Welcome to our house," Pa said, and he managed a thin smile and shook her hand. He turned to me. "What is matter you stand with mouth hang down? You never see girl before? And you . . ." He motioned brusquely to Mike. "Go look at turkey and tell Simonakis and Father Kontoyannis be ready to eat."

Mike hesitated for just a moment. His jaw worked hard silently and then he clamped his mouth tight and started to the kitchen pulling off his coat on the way.

"This son is Tony," Pa said.

"Hello, Sheila," I said.

She smiled at me then and her teeth were even and white like chalk. "Mike has told me about Tony," she said. Pa took her coat, and she unknotted and removed the babushka I did not like and her hair was the color of brown taffy and fell in soft clusters about her ears. I got a funny tight curling in my stomach.

"You come sit down," Pa said. "Tony bring glass of wine."

They walked together into the parlor. She wore a slim dark suit, and her legs in silk stockings were slender and her ankles were trim. I went for the glasses and the wine and met Mike on the way from the kitchen.

"What's Pa saying to her?"

"He's all right," I said. "Don't worry. He won't say anything wrong."

"He'd better not," Mike said, and his big fists were clenched as he walked to the parlor. He was my brother and yet at that moment he seemed a stranger. Maybe that was what loving a woman did to a man.

In the kitchen Father Kontoyannis and Simonakis were just finishing their glasses of wine.

"The Irish are beer drinkers," Simonakis said. "From generation to generation, they have been watered down."

"There is nothing wrong with good beer," I said.

Simonakis snorted. "Beer is for the belly," he said. "Wine is for wisdom."

I placed the bottle and several glasses on a tray and turned to go back inside.

"What happened to you?" I said.

He curled his lip and spoke to the priest.

"Once I told this snot stories," he said. "Now he becomes more like his big brother every day. Arrogance and disrespect."

"If you speak of the Irish before Mike," I said, "he will probably give you arrogance and disrespect across the head."

"Come to church Sunday, Spiro," Father Kontoyannis said with a gleam in his eye. "We will pray together for the salvation of the arrogant and disrespectful young."

"Do you want me in church too?" I asked.

He laughed and shook his head.

"No hurry about you," he said. "The saints spend the first forty years of their lives carousing and enjoying themselves, and when the edge of their appetites has worn off, they repent and rest. You still have time."

"That's a powerful moral you draw, Father," I said.

"We live in powerful times," he said.

In a few moments we sat down at the holiday table. Pa carved the turkey and I carried the tray of cranberries and bread from the kitchen and Mike poured the wine. Father Kontoyannis said grace, and once in the middle of the prayer he stopped and looked ominously at Simonakis, who was already chewing on an olive. Simonakis shrugged and stopped.

The dinner was not too festive. Once started, the conversation had a way of dying into silence. Father Kontoyannis was calm and friendly as always and kept us in balance. But Pa ate silently and Mike was tense. Only Simonakis ate lustily, stuffing in the turkey and dressing as if he had heard rumors the world was going to end and only the big eaters would be spared. In between shovels of food, he drank zealously of his wine.

"More turkey for girl," Pa said. "Mike, pass platter. More dressing . . . Tony, get dressing."

She shook her head and it made the taffy-colored hair tremble about her cheeks. I felt the strange unrest again.

"More wine for girl," Pa said. "One more glass."

Pa was not a hypocrite. He had not wanted the girl in his house but now she was at his table. Hospitality, which is like a religion to a Greek, at least a Greek like Pa, demanded that a guest be well taken care of.

I filled her glass from the decanter of wine. She thanked me and for a moment I saw her eyes. I think she sensed the tension and was trying very hard not to let it show.

"Maybe she prefers beer?" Simonakis asked.

Mike glared at him and started to speak. Father Kontoyannis broke in quickly.

"Mike, I will have a little more turkey, please," he said.

Mike looked murder at Simonakis and passed the platter of turkey to the priest.

"Good beer is nothing to poke fun at," Mike said.

Simonakis stared at him with pity.

"The drinking of wine is more than swallowing for

thirst," he said. "It is a ceremony of the earth. First the grapes grow heavy on the vines and then they are plucked. The crushing by the young maidens. Finally the casks in cool cellars."

"When my father was alive," Sheila said, "he felt that way about good Irish whiskey and about the Shannon."

"What is this Shannon?" Simonakis asked.

"That is a river," Father Kontoyannis said, "a river in Ireland."

Sheila smiled. "My father used to say the Shannon was more than a river. The Shannon was Ireland."

"Sheila's ma and pa were killed together in an auto accident," Mike said, "a few years ago while they were driving West on a vacation."

Father Kontoyannis shook his head slowly and a sudden shadow crossed his cheeks. " A terrible thing to lose both at once," he said gently to Sheila.

Sheila started to say something and then paused and looked at Pa. "For a little while I did not want to live," she said, "but time passes and you change."

"Do you have other brothers or sisters?" I asked.

"I have a married brother in Milwaukee," she said. "He works in a brewery there."

Simonakis made a face but did not speak.

Pa raised his glass and we all followed suit. He looked at Sheila and then at Mike.

"Peace and love in our house," he said, and his face was sober and a little pale. Sheila raised her glass to her lips, looking at Mike, and he was watching her, and the two of them drank in almost the same breath and as if the rest of us were not there.

At the end of the meal, Sheila wanted to help carry the plates into the kitchen. Pa would not let her.

"We do dishes any time," he said. "Now we sit and digest food. Mike, bring more wood for fire."

"I'll show you our house," I said, "but walk lightly because the floors aren't very sturdy."

Mike stopped on his way to get the wood. "We got a good view too. On a very clear day you can see the house next door."

Pa's face darkened slightly.

"Sons are comics," he said. "House that keep rain and cold from their heads is big joke."

"We weren't making jokes, Pa," I said. "We were just kidding."

"They call this area around the mills the bush," Father Kontoyannis said. "Perhaps because the houses are tangled closely like trees in a forest. But I have been in many of these homes. The people are strong with love and respect for one another."

We all stood silent for a moment and Mike left the room and Sheila took my arm.

"I would like to see the house," she said.

We didn't speak going up the stairs. I showed her my room and then Mike's room. She peeked in his closet and laughed a little at the way his shoes and dirty clothes were piled. She stopped laughing and looked sorry and picked up a shirt to hang on the back of the door.

"You need a woman in this house," she said. I resented that because it seemed to criticize Pa. He had always been enough for the big things, the things that mattered.

We walked to the big room at the end of the hall. The room that belonged to Ma and Pa when she was alive. I opened the door and reached in and snapped the switch. Sheila stood in the doorway and caught her breath. For a long moment she stood there without moving.

It was a room in which all the objects were carriers of a strange air of untouched and ageless serenity. The dark chairs before the ceiling-to-floor window, the still sheer curtains, the great bed postered in swirls of glistening wood all seemed to repel time and reject reflection. As if the room were a valley sheltered and hidden between the crests of high mountains.

"It's beautiful," she said. "Mike told me about this room. I had to see it to realize how beautiful it really is."

I walked to the foot of the postered bed with the regal canopy of lace. I rubbed my fingers gently across the fine dark-grained wood.

"This bed was made for Ma and Pa by an old Greek furniture maker when they were married. He was very old and is now dead, but he would come to visit just to see it again. He used to say it was the most beautiful thing he had ever done."

She walked slowly around the bed and fingered the fringe of fine lace.

"After Ma died, Pa would not stay in here and moved into the bedroom down the hall. He left everything belonging to her here."

"It's like a shrine," Sheila said.

"All her clothes are still in the closet," I said. "The wedding linens and laces from her mother. The wedding garland and the wedding candles and an ikon from the church. All of that is here."

"He must have loved her very much," she said.

I stood silent for a moment and almost as sharp as pain felt the familiar warmth. In this great bed, like a page from an Old Testament psalm, my parents had loved. Within these walls I came in blood to life and light.

Sheila watched me and I felt a sudden uneasiness under her eyes.

"You love this room," she said. "You love your father and the memories in this house."

I felt a quick little pinch of anger because she had so easily touched the bone beneath my flesh.

"Mike loves this house," I said. "We both love Pa."

She shook her head slowly, persisting. "He loves this house and your father, but not like you. You stand in this room as if it is a church and you watch your father sometimes as if it hurts to take your eyes away." She came closer and touched my arm gently. "There is nothing wrong with loving very much. I loved my father and mother like that. Not as deeply as you perhaps, but still very much." For a moment the remembered grief reclaimed her voice and cheeks and then was gone. "I love Mike like that."

I didn't know what to say. I felt loyalty to Pa and what he wanted for us. I was sorry for her too.

"I want to be part of your family," she said, and she spoke in almost a whisper. "I want to belong with you and your father and with Mike."

I turned away so she would not see my face. I was sorry for her and yet angry with her as well.

I walked out of the room and stopped outside the door. When I reached in to close the light, she followed me out. The hallway was dim and shadowed, with only a small night light burning at the other end. I should have taken her arm, but in some strange way I wanted to hurt her just a little. I started walking alone.

I heard Mike calling us from the foot of the stairs. Then I was ashamed and turned back, but she had slowly made her own way. At the head of the stairs there was light to guide her and she no longer needed me. I waited and she passed me silently and walked down to Mike.

Late that night it snowed again. I did not feel like sleeping and sat for a while watching the snow fall outside the window of my room. Mike had taken Sheila home and had not yet returned.

I left the room and went quietly down the hall. In the kitchen downstairs I opened the icebox and got the milk and took a box of crackers off the pantry shelf. I sat at the table and tasted the salty crackers and drank the cold milk.

I heard the stairs creaking and a moment later Pa came into the kitchen. He wore his old cotton bathrobe with the cord trailing on the floor. He stood blinking in the light.

"What hell is matter with you?" he said.

"Your snoring kept me awake."

He laughed. "You crazy . . . I never snore my life."

He poured himself a glass of milk and sat down across from me at the table. He looked up at the clock above the stove.

"Not home yet," he said. "What hell do this late with girl?"

"Maybe they went to a show," I said. "Shows let out late."

We fell silent and I could hear the snow cracking softly against the window.

"Tony," he said slowly. "Tony, you think Mike want marry this girl?"

I stared into the glass feeling a sudden tightness in my throat.

"She's a pretty girl, Pa," I said. "Maybe he likes her because she is pretty."

He made an impatient gesture with his hands.

"Damn pretty fine for bed. Other things more important."

He was staring off at the window and I saw the lines of age that had begun to scar his cheeks and pouch the flesh around his eyes. He was a lion that was getting old and the sadness of that wrenched through my flesh.

"She is not Greek," he said, and he shook his head slowly, heavily. "Maybe she good girl, but she is from different people." He paused and drew a deep and labored breath. "When Mama was alive, we talk of boys someday marry. All her things belong then to women you and Mike take for wife. I do not give Mama's things to woman who cannot understand."

"Maybe Sheila understands, Pa. Maybe she doesn't have to be Greek to understand about the family."

"She understand we are Greek family?" The words pulled tightly from between his teeth. "She understand that in years Mike gone in war I pray thousand prayers and light thousand candles he come back my house? I pray he come back so I see him marry and father own sons. She understand these things, then why she not leave him alone?"

I heard the key suddenly in the back door and it swung open. Mike stood there a moment and seemed surprised to find Pa and me up. Then he shook off the snow and stepped inside. He took off his hat and coat and hung them behind the door.

"What hell you do this late?" Pa said and his voice shook a little under the effort to speak quietly.

Mike's face was set in hard lines and he spoke straight at Pa.

"I was with my girl," he said. "I was out with my girl."

"Nice girl," Pa said. "Out with man after two in morning."

Mike's eyes flashed and he started to say something and then looked at me. He turned and without a word walked out of the kitchen. A few seconds later, we heard him on the stairs.

Pa sat there before his unfinished glass of milk. I closed the box of crackers and put the glasses in the sink.

"Let's go to bed, Pa," I said. "You got to get up for early shift in the morning."

He stood up and his big shoulders were slumped a little under his robe and his cheeks were pale. Then his mouth loosened in a pensive smile and he gave my chin an easy shove with his hand.

We walked up the stairs and said good night to one another and went to our rooms.

I got into bed and lay shivering for a while listening to the silent house. I could feel Pa and Mike awake in their beds staring into the darkness. For a moment I yearned again for the lost years of growing up. Years when Pa still tucked us into bed and listened to our prayers and we felt the rough needles of his cheek and smelled the mill dust on his clothes.

But we could not go back. Mike had found his woman. Pa lay hurt in the darkness. I did not know what was right.

I only knew something had come to pass and our house would never be the same again.

Chapter 2

IT WAS LATE MORNING WHEN I WOKE. I FELT THE light pressing against my eyes and I turned my face away from the windows and squinted at the room. The walls of flower-printed paper and the desk and the bookcase full of books and the pants and shirt across the back of the chair were flooded with daylight reflected brightly off the snow and streaming in through the windows.

I did not want to get up. I was warm and lazy under the blankets and pleasurably aware of my body.

The house was silent. Pa had left early for his shift. Perhaps Mike was still asleep. As a child I could remember waking in the morning to the clatter of pans and dishes from the kitchen, familiar sounds that urged me out of bed.

If Ma was not dead the kitchen would not be hushed.

30

Maybe then I would want to get up and go downstairs. I shut my eyes tightly and tried to imagine what she would look like standing in the kitchen with the sunlight on her face. Her hair had been almost dark and swept back behind her ears and pinned into a bun. Would it have become gray now like Pa's hair? Her body had been small and slim-boned as the body of a girl. It is strange that I should remember her small when I was so young and small myself. Perhaps Pa's broad big body beside her made me remember her that way. Would her figure still have been as spare of flesh or would the years have padded her about the waist and hips?

If Mike married Sheila and she came to live with us, there would be a woman in our house again. Would she cook and care for all of us? I tried to imagine her in the kitchen in the morning, bare-legged with a wrapper around her ungirdled body and the taffy-colored hair lovely about her cheeks and her lips still pale with the color of sleep.

I turned over on my stomach. I put my face into my pillow and pressed the length of my body hard against the mattress. Sheila had rounded and secret breasts and her throat rose gracefully from the shadowed cleft between them. Sheila had slender legs, soft looking and shining in silk stockings.

Damn all girls with secret breasts and slender legs. How lovely they were. Sheila had legs like Angela. Slender and shining legs like the legs of Angela.

31

Angela. Angela. Someone play that name again.

No, first there was Frances. Funny how I could not think of Angela without remembering Frances. Maybe without Frances to educate my darkness I would not have appreciated Angela. They were as different as summer and winter. Frances had broad shoulders and scaled cheeks and martial breasts and the stride of a martinet.

Before Frances I never had much to do with girls except for coke dates and some dances in high school. I wanted to have more to do with girls. All through the years of school, however, they seemed to divide between the younger giddy ones who giggled too much and the older ones with whom I could not catch up. When I got my varsity letter in basketball in my last year at high school, things got a little better. I double-dated with other fellows on the team and sprawled in the back seat of cars with girls who snuggled close and had warm restless lips. When we stopped necking and had to talk, I didn't know what to say. The war was in its last year, although I did not know it then, and Mike was overseas. He had written Pa and me after Tarawa and his letters did not say much, but I saw newsreels of the beaches of that island strewn with dead, and the bodies floating face down in the water, and the charred and blackened forms of what had once been men in the bunkers after the flame throwers had passed. I felt the fury and horror of what was taking place across the earth and I wanted to do my share with Mike and ease his burden, and yet, I was afraid and secretly glad I was still too young. I marked the passing of days, uneasy and voiceless about many things I felt like frenzy in my bones. But the girls just giggled and snuggled closer and raised their warm restless lips to be kissed. I kissed them too, but they did not appease my unrest. Even though I marveled at the soft clearness of their skin, and the way their bright and golden legs flashed as they ran up stairs to classes or the lithe half-dancing way they walked and shrieked in secretive pairs.

The war finished with Hiroshima and Nagasaki, and Mike was on his way home. I was a freshman in college and unprepared for Frances when I first met her. She was the most vociferous voice in the economics class of Mr. Waugh. He was a weary-faced man who did not seem able to generate any enthusiasm for what he taught. I guess he felt the war had bred nothing but confusion and chaos. He did the best he could with us. In the middle of his lecture, Frances would boom out like a cannon. Adam Smith was defunct. Parson Malthus was gloomy. Mr. Waugh would shake his head slowly. "Frances," he would say, "Frances, would you mind not shouting your comments. If there is disorder in the world, it does not follow there must be disorder in this class." Frances would clamp her lips shut and glare about the room trying to pin down the source of muted giggles. For a few moments she would remain silent until something again

33

lit her fuse and she waved her arms vigorously. If she were not called on almost at once, she could not restrain herself and boomed her great voice again about the room.

I admired Frances. I did not mind she was a little taller than me and broader in the shoulders. I did not mind the blackheads on her nose or the flat tasteless gray shoes on her feet that looked bigger than my own. More important than any of this, she shouted what was for me a new and fascinating philosophy of history. There were phrases like "dialectical materialism" and "surplus value" and a fierce prophet named Karl Marx whom Frances ranked several floors above Jesus Christ and Mohammed. She painted a bright new world in which all men would be equal and share equally the fruits of their labor. Thus, if all men were equal, there would be no need for future wars. I did not completely understand, but I accepted a good deal of what Frances said on faith. I became her disciple. Right into my sophomore year, Frances carried me around like a marsupial carrying her young.

One evening, after hearing a lecture on the Utopian Socialists by a visiting professor from Princeton, we walked a little on campus and sat on the stairs of the physics building. It was a night in October, pensive with the memories of half-forgotten autumns. It was the night of the Dance Frolic in Beecher Hall, and the sounds of distant music and laughter carried clearly across the darkness.

Frances had finally stopped talking and we sat quietly and listened. I don't remember what I was thinking when I felt her leg pressed against my own. She was breathing hard and her strong face, half hidden in shadows, was tight and a little desperate and she made funny choking sounds deep in her throat. Then, without a word, she grabbed me and kissed me. I struggled, but Frances had the arms of a discus thrower, and I felt her mouth as if a suction cup had been clamped over my lips. I could almost hear her booming voice and my head began to swim and I gave a mighty wrench and tore loose. Then I was off the stairs and half running through the October night, warm with the memories of half-forgotten autumns and the music of the Frolic sweet and wild upon the darkness.

I stopped running about a block away. I stood and gave the matter serious thought. My running seemed ridiculous. I had not considered Comrade Frances just another girl, but I admired her enough, so if she felt the warm night and the coming Autumn and wanted me to kiss her, I just might do so. I went back a bit warily, but Frances was gone.

The next morning in class she cut me dead. Her face was sterner than usual and when she popped out of her seat, she shouted much louder than she ever had before, and Mr. Waugh was in despair. At the end of class, I tried to catch her eye but she pointedly ignored me and walked out of the room engaged in heated conversation with Ralph Nowak, who was tall and wore glasses and fervently admired John Maynard Keynes.

A few days later, she scribbled me a cursory note and flipped it on my desk as she walked by. She wrote she had tested me. I was not worthy to stand beside her on the barricades. I was a lousy reactionary. She wanted her copy of *Das Kapital* back at once. I tore up her note and gave her back everything.

I made up my mind I would never again become intellectually involved with any girl.

I rolled over and over on the bed and the blankets twisted tightly around me. Through the closed window I could hear the shrieking of children playing in the snow. In the distance I could hear the furnaces of the mills like the pulsing of a mighty heart. Like the pulsing of my own heart when I remembered Angela.

Angela. Angela. Someone play that name again.

She sat a chair ahead of me in biology. She had long, gleaming blonde hair that curled about the back of her neck and made study of amoebas and crustaceans ridiculous. The rest of us might have evolved from one-celled creatures, but not Angela. She had a mouth as round and full as a plum and languid legs and a body all delicate and soft and powdered. She read confession magazines and pulp love stories hidden between the covers

36

of her notebook. She attended school only to mark time until the opportunity presented itself for her to make a proper marriage. She fancied herself the wife of some business tycoon who would take her to the Riviera for an extended honeymoon and forever after let her lounge upon a satin-sheeted bed of love. To this union, she consecrated her virginity. She invited praise and amorous attention and gave small warm favors in return, but her virtue was a promissory note she had still not signed. In spite of this obstacle, we battled for her favors. I had come a long way since Frances and hurled myself into the thick of the fight. To my surprise, I found myself in the exalted inner circle. It wasn't until later I realized our classroom seating arrangement and my good average were the price of admission. From my chair I could pass her test answers with less chance of detection than from any other chair in the room. In addition I did her homework for her.

When I kissed other girls it was pleasant and tingling. When I kissed Angela it was like coming close to a blazing furnace and peeping in the door. Angela burned with a white-hot flame under the powder and softness.

Sometimes we studied together at her house. Rather, I did both our work carefully while she read her magazines. Her father was in the wholesale clothing business, a little man with a dark peaked face and pants that bagged around his skinny rump. Her mother was a tall and bony woman with her hands reddened from years of wash and dishes. Sometimes, when we were sitting together, I caught them watching Angela. They both looked bewildered.

One night I borrowed the car from Mike and took Angela to the Sophomore Cotillion. She was in shimmering white and I was proud and possessed. She danced all night with the varsity football team, big hulking clods who held her too close. Angela had received bountiful attentions before, but never with such concentrated vigor. They spiked her punch and clipped locks of her hair as souvenirs. Her libido was set aflame from the heat of a dozen passes. Then a fight started in a far corner of the floor and the varsity rushed to mix in. They left Angela like some forgotten Ophelia. In the confusion I got her out and into the car. I drove off fast while she slumped in the seat singing softly to herself and murmuring the name of Richard — he was a big blonde tackle with a crew cut.

I did not drive straight home but parked in a deserted stretch of park by the lake. She came willingly into my arms and burned where I touched her. I remembered my countless humiliations and fondled her roughly and accepted all her furious responses as if they were for me alone. She bit my lips and scratched my cheeks and made me more fiercely aware of my body than I had ever been.

I had never taken a girl before. Besides that, all my knowledge of front seat gymnastics was hearsay. But I guess somehow or other I would have done it then because she wanted me to and would have helped me where she could. I wanted her at that moment more than I had ever wanted anything, but it was no good. She was still a little drunk and I knew she thought she was with Richard and if those were not enough, I remembered her vision of virtue until she entered marriage. I pushed her over and took her home.

I was sorry afterwards. I never got another chance. Shortly after that night she left school and went West and one of the girls to whom she had written later said she had been married to some Pasadena tycoon who owned a chain of theaters. She didn't get to go to the Riviera on her honeymoon after all. They went to Hawaii. I never did find out if the sheets were satin, but I often wonder if the tycoon she married knew what I had done for them. Damn him and Angela too.

I had to get up. Between Frances and Angela, my bed had suddenly gotten crowded. I untwisted myself out of the blankets and went to the bath. The stream of the shower felt good across my body, cleanly washing away the adhesive past. Afterwards, I dressed and went down to the kitchen. Mike was drinking a cup of coffee at the table.

"Morning, Duke," Mike said. "I thought maybe you wanted lunch in bed."

"All right," I said. "Don't make a fuss about it."

He smiled and I looked at his face in that moment as

if I were seeing it through Sheila's eyes, not handsome, but brown and strong, and the kind of face a woman would like.

"Well," he said and he leaned forward in his chair.

"Well what?" I asked, making it innocent.

He pushed his coffee cup away and hooted.

"You know the hell about what," he said. "What did you think of Sheila?"

I paused in front of the stove and made a fierce face and waved my hands vigorously.

"The Rose of Sharon and the Lily of the Valley!" I said. "Salome and Bathsheba rolled into one!"

"You punk!" he laughed. "You're just jealous. You don't know what to say when you meet a real woman."

"She is a change," I said. "Up to now the only women you knew had to have monthly physicals."

He made a lunge for me, but over the years I had learned to be quick. I made it out of the kitchen before he could clear the table. He sat down again, and I went back warily to continue fixing my eggs.

"What did the old man say about Sheila last night?" he asked.

"Nothing much," I said carefully. "He was a little worried because you were out late."

"Sure," Mike snickered. "Worried because I wasn't out with some damn Greek wench he would have approved."

"You got to see the old man's side," I said. "The

way he thinks and believes. You can't get him to change all at once."

"I don't want to change him," Mike said. "He's okay as he is except about this business of being Greek. That crap goes in the old country but over here it's different. The war made it different. I'm almost twenty-six years old. I found a girl I want to marry. I want him to climb off my back with his load of history."

"Give him time," I said. "Jesus, Mike, give him a little time."

"Time for what?" Mike said, and his voice rose a little. "Ever since we were kids we eat and sleep and grow on the glory of Greece. All around us we got nuts like Simonakis haughty as hell because two thousand years ago they knocked hell out of some Persians and knocked hell out of each other and a guy named Socrates got poisoned and a guy named Odysseus got lost."

"That's history," I said. "Everybody's got the right to be a little proud of their history."

He shrugged. "Okay, let's forget the history. I'm not asking his blessing now so I can rob a bank or steal out of the church collection plate. I only want to get married to a nice respectable American girl of Irish extraction. Does that make me crazy?"

"He wants you to get married," I said. "Someday he wants me to get married too. He wants everybody to get married."

He had to laugh at that and shook his head.

"My kid brother," he said. "Sophomore diplomat. Adviser to Mr. Truman."

"You're a big blow," I said. "You are as much for the old man as me."

"Sure," Mike said. "I'm for him, but I'm for my own life too. The old man worked double shifts through the war and practiced going down to the basement during air-raid drills and didn't notice that the world was being changed." He got up and put his breakfast dishes in the sink. "Wash these when you're through with your own."

"That's all I seem to be doing lately," I said. "Washing dishes."

"I'm going to retape that wire in the basement," he said.

"Okay," I said. "I guess I'll go out for a little while."

"Where you going?"

"Gerontis'," I said.

"Keep hanging out in there," he shook his head warningly, "You'll become like Simonakis and the rest of those coffeehouse bums."

He went down the back stairs into the basement. I finished my coffee and placed my dishes in the sink with Mike's and left them unwashed. I put on my jacket and left the house.

The ground outside was covered with snow through which half-buried ash cans and wire trash burners stuck up. I followed the big prints of Pa's shoes all the way to the alley and had room to spare.

I got to the corner and turned down Dart Street. The air was brisk and sharp across my cheeks. A gust of wind swept the snow in drifts against the fronts of stores. A few stocky wives of mill men, bundled in cloth coats and babushkas walked wearily into the Polish and Greek and Italian groceries with children pulling at their tails. The taverns were open for beer and sausage lunches, and the jukeboxes beat to the street.

Gerontis' was a coffeehouse and tavern next to the pool hall on Dart Street, the gathering place all through the day and far into the night of the old Greek mill men and produce men and shopkeepers. Here they could sit among the tables with their own and sip from the little glasses of masticha or cups of sweet coffee. They would sometimes play pastra or koltsina but most often just talk of the old country across the ocean.

I liked to sit and listen to them reminisce of the mountains they had left and the sea breezes taking the fishing boats out in the early morning. Sometimes, they refought the battles of Ancient Greece and relived the sweep of glory when Greek vanquished mighty Persian. Their voices shook with woe as they mourned the war between Athens and Sparta which bled both states to death. When they were not orating in the manner of Pericles, they were philosophizing in the manner of Socrates seeking an answer to the meaning of truth. In a way I guess Mike

43

was right. Many of them were pompous and arrogant and would not have known the truth if it had teeth and bit them on the ass.

I stood inside the door and for a few moments, after the brightness of the street, the room seemed dark as night. But even in darkness I heard the familiar rise and fall of many voices, and I would have known where I was by the rank smell of old pipes and sharp cigars and sweet smell of the syrupy coffee that drifted like a thick mist out of the gloom.

Somebody called to me from a table near the door. I looked hard and recognized Chris Bizakis, a friend of Mike's who worked at the Universal. He was sitting alone with a cigar in his mouth. I walked to his table. He reached up and pulled the tip of his heavy mustache in greeting.

"Nice to see you," I said.

"Same here," he said. "Where's the brother?"

"Taping a wire."

He shook his head sadly.

"What a damn bore it must be to own a house. All I ever want is a suitcase."

I saw the gleaming bald head of Simonakis in a group of men a few tables away. He saw me at the same time and made a sharp snap of his fingers in the air in greeting. On his right was some man with a name I did not know, but he had a nose like a small mountain and when he lifted the glass of masticha to his mouth it disappeared under the peak. Beside him there was Uncle Demetri, who was nobody's uncle but for some reason was called uncle by everyone. There was Volakis, who had sold the Icarian grocery to Karpetsou, who was my Pa's best man, and Camberos, who had a sad lined face and spent all of his days and most of his nights right here in the coffeehouse. A few years back he had journeyed to the old country and returned with a wife thirty years younger than himself. Painfully, he taught her to speak English as broken as his own so she could help him in the candy store. She spoke well enough in the end to understand a young Swedish sailor off one of the lake ore boats and run off with him. After that, Camberos made the coffeehouse his home.

There were others whose names I did not know but whose faces I had seen a hundred times, old men whose voices blended into a chorus of dark omen and lamentation at having left the land of their birth.

In the evening, when Pantaris came from the west side with his lyre, the old men would dance, leap in a weird and powerful return to the past, becoming figures from another age. Furious old men, whose lives were aimless in the daylight, given purpose and direction in the shrill night. The shadows ran up and down the walls then and the music came like fire from all corners of the room. At moments such as those, I tasted the fruit that nourished Pa and found it sweet and filling in my mouth.

Simonakis rose from his chair and in a loud fierce voice called to Gerontis for more masticha. The old men beat their fists on the table in agreement.

"Our glasses have been empty for ten minutes," Simonakis shouted. "This service is not fit for Turks, let alone lions." The old men beat their fists and hissed the service of Gerontis.

The swinging door from the kitchen opened and a waiter with a great handlebar mustache came through, carrying two bottles on a tray. He wore a white apron around his slim waist and the delicate tips of his mustache curled disdainfully toward the ceiling.

A second waiter, small and sweating, wiped our table and I ordered coffee.

"The old boys are in high spirits today," Chris said. "They have been rumbling like volcanoes for an hour."

The lean waiter had swiftly filled their glasses and Simonakis raised his glass high. The old men followed and raised their own.

"To the day of the lion," Simonakis said, "and against the night of the jackal and the wolf."

The old men beat their fists and sipped their masticha. Simonakis sat down and Uncle Demetri stood up. He waved his glass and tried vainly to match the fierceness of Simonakis.

"It is from the Greek that man has learned to accept the truth as good and beauty as the eye of God."

Before he could sit down, Volakis, the Icarian, jumped

up. In his eagerness to be heard, he got his feet twisted and nearly fell. Simonakis and Uncle Demetri helped to steady him. Finally set, he raised his glass and wobbled it in the air. The waiter standing nearby fixed him with a cold stare.

"This next summer," Volakis said. "I will go home. I will see my village and walk along the sea as I did when I was a boy. Drink in good health to my trip."

The old men beat their fists and cheered and drank to Volakis.

This pledge to go home I had heard spoken to the waving of glasses of masticha countless times. The older ones swore more fiercely of making the journey as if knowing they were in a race with death. Even Pa, on those still nights of the full moon when pale reflections made him restless, promised to go back and see again the land of his birth.

Somehow, this journey was made by few. Money might be short or health infirm. Perhaps, in a way, they were unwilling to admit even to each other they were afraid. From a distance and over the years only the peaks of mountains golden in the sun could be seen across the seas. If they returned and found the land without adornment and the reality barren beside the dream, they would have nothing left.

The waiter looked at Volakis, and he was a dry-cheeked, new breed of Greek who had come over since the war. He rubbed his nose and twirled the tips of his

47

mustache and shook his head, scornful of their boastings.

"You had best stay here," he said. "You go home and find rocks and children with rags on their feet and dry dead vines in the orchards."

Volakis looked at him in sudden anger, and his jaw muscles worked silently as if a stone had been popped into his mouth.

"You are an idiot!" he said. "You live in the dark! I go home because I was born there, and after forty years I wish to see the land once more before I die." He finished and spit on the floor.

The old men beat their fists and hooted ridicule upon the waiter. He stood against them all, his face stern and combative, holding his lean hips between his hands.

"I am not an idiot," he said. "You are the idiot to go back now." He looked at the others and swept his hands in a gesture of contempt before their ignorance. "He will find nothing the same," he said. "The war has changed everything. The villages resemble the ruined temples. The fields are black and desolate. The orphans walk across rubble and new graves scratching for food."

The old men complained noisily, and Simonakis raised his hand, and they became still. Volakis sat down, and the waiter cleared his throat and waited.

Simonakis stood up and for a long moment watched the waiter in silence.

"This goat," he said slowly, and the way he spoke, that word consigned the waiter to massive disgrace, "this goat that works here because he is related to the wife of Gerontis, this goat was in Greece when the Nazi barbarians came. He ran to the mountains and hid beneath the rocks."

The waiter stood suddenly outraged, and the great mustache bristled above his lips.

"You lie!" he shouted. "I fought while you, old bones, sat and drank masticha and farted in your chairs." He snorted with anger. "We fought with knives against guns and with old muskets against the diving planes. When we had nothing left to fight with, they killed us like sheep being slaughtered; we ran to save the few lives left."

Simonakis bent a little and pounded on the table.

"You see!" he cried. "You see!" He looked around in triumph. "You see what sense he makes!" He looked at the waiter and an ice-crowned glare darkened his face. "You say that Greek warriors ran." He shook his head slowly and with solemn measure. "Only the goats ran. The men stayed and fought. They died perhaps like the men of Leonidas at Thermopylae, but they did not run."

The old men beat their fists on the table and whistled through meager lips and spit for the goats who ran.

The waiter tried to catch his breath. He was no longer calm, and anger had robbed him of effective speech. Simonakis waited without pity to return to the attack.

49

"You think life is a glass of masticha," the waiter said finally. "Let me tell you there are no heroes . . . not then or not now, in the old country nor any place else. There are only desperate men."

"No heroes!" Simonakis said, and his bald head stiffened like the head of a fighting cock that had just been spiked. The old men held their breaths before such blasphemy. "You say no heroes?" Simonakis said. "No heroes in the land watered with the blood of countless warriors? Are you a Turk? Is your head on straight or do I call for help?"

I sat beside Chris and watched and listened. I sipped my coffee and in a way could sympathize with the stricken waiter because he was probably right. Yet, somewhere deep inside my blood, a part of me wished that he was not right. The war had changed everything, he said. Mike told me that too. But the war had not bound the agitated spirit of the old men. From some inexhaustible source, known only to themselves, they drew on clear springs of faith.

The waiter stood tense and silent wondering how to retreat. The old men stared their contempt and waited for Simonakis to execute the kill.

"Listen," Simonakis said slowly, and he spoke the word as if it unveiled a bronze monument to the past. "Where you find Greeks you will find heroes. Because there is something heroic and eternal about the land which nourishes their roots. Look back. They came into a world of darkness. Look back. They changed the destiny of man." He spoke fervently as if he were reciting a prayer. He spoke to all of us and his voice trembled. "Our land is poor now and swept by the ravages of war, but we are not defeated. Even the ruins beckon us to hold our faith. Our spirit is winged and eternal."

When he finished, the old men did not bang their fists and shout. They nodded sagely, quietly in agreement, secure in the glory of the past. This was their reality. The Golden Age was not a song for poets or a page in a book of history but a godhead which they worshiped as eternal and carried with them across the world.

I stood up to leave. With a sudden depression I understood what this came to in our family. Pa held to the past, and Mike pulled to the future. I stood on a bridge between.

"Stick around," Chris said. "The volcanoes erupt every hour on the hour."

"I can't stand the blood."

I paid Gerontis for the coffee and left Simonakis and the old men in the shadows muttering quietly to themselves after the passing of the storm.

Back home, Mike still worked in the basement. I washed the dishes and pulled the salami and cheese from the icebox and made myself a sandwich and made sandwiches for Mike's lunchbox and fresh coffee for his Thermos. Pa's shift finished at three in the afternoon and Mike's shift started then.

Afterwards, I went to my room and to my desk. I fingered some of the books I should study. History and philosophy and political science. One more year to my degree. Then to stand before a class of students in some high school and talk of the histories of men and nations. The prospect excited me and yet frightened me too. During practice-teaching sessions in the last month, I had witnessed the unconcealed amusement of the students as we took our turns before them. They seemed riotous and without faith in what we wanted to do.

I worried sometimes that I was going into teaching because Pa wanted it so much. With other fathers, it was medicine or law, but Pa had the veneration of the Greek for the teacher. I had worked one summer in the mill, in the Universal as a stocker, and if Pa and Mike had left me alone, I think I would have been content to stay. In the evening my lunchbox was packed with theirs, and when we worked the same shifts, we walked to the mills together. We walked past the blast furnaces and the Bessemers, and past the long trains of flatcars with the bright orange slabs cooling in the night. In the morning, after the long night turn, we stopped wearily in Gerontis' for masticha and the rousing black coffee. The place would be warm and alive with men off the midnight shift, and we drank and laughed together, and I swear to God that was where I felt I belonged. But my suggestion that I remain in the mills brought outrage and anger from Pa and Mike. They wanted me beyond the flame and fury of the furnaces, a Varinakis with knowledge, a man of books and ideas. How could I tell them that I would have been grateful to have spent my life working beside them, the three of us together as we had always been.

I went back to the books and picked up Fletcher Pratt's *Ordeal By Fire*. I opened the book to the page with marker where I had last stopped reading.

Up from the south, huge and menacing, rolled Lee and his 80,000. He slid west along the rivers; on June 12, rebel cavalry was reported in the Shenandoah Valley. Milroy, whom Jackson beat among the hills the year before, had 11,000 men at Winchester. Pugnacious Milroy, when scouts brought the news of Lee's advance, he thought it a raid and stayed to fight. . . .

Rebel cavalry rode through the passes of the Blue Ridge; a reconnaissance showed there were still Confederates at Fredericksburg. "If the head of Lee's army," Lincoln wrote down to Hooker, "is at Winchester and the tail at Fredericksburg, the animal must be very slim somewhere. Could you not break him?" "Impossible," said Hooker. "I cannot divine his intentions as long as he fills the country with a cloud of cavalry."

I tried to read on, but I started thinking about Simonakis and the old men. In Ancient Greece more than two thousand years ago, men fought and watered the earth with their blood and sang the praises of the gods who made them Greeks and not barbarians. At Fredericksburg and at Shiloh and at Manassas, men long dead proved to what earth and faith they owed allegiance. Mike fought at Tarawa on the blistered beaches among the bodies floating face down in the water, and in the end at least knew where he belonged.

Where did I belong? How much of me belonged to Pa and Simonakis and the old men who kept their faith among the ruins, and how much of me belonged to Mike and the men of Shiloh and this land on which I grew.

A little before three o'clock, I walked with Mike to the south gate. Across the fences, the great gabled roofs of the mills cloaked under snow stretched for miles. A burning haze hung in the air. The hissing roar of the furnaces and the furious clatter of the steel across the rolls beat together like wind and thunder. In the distance across the river, the haze was suddenly shattered by the brilliance of a Bessemer in blow.

The shifts were changing. The men came out the gate alone or in groups, some with their heads up and laughing and others wearily staring at the ground.

About a half-mile away, the other side of the fence, I saw Pa coming down the hill at the head of his crew from the plate mill. That was how I remembered him when, as a child, I waited inside the gate in the guard's shanty and he would come striding down the hill. I would run out to meet him, and he would swing me into the air and kiss me and perch me on his shoulders. I would walk among the mill men, taller than any of them, feeling his big hands holding me secure. They would call me Big Angelo's boy and would slap my legs.

When Pa passed the shanty and saw us, he waved and walked through the gate and came to where we stood. Mike was staring a little sullenly at the ground. Pa glanced quickly at him and then turned to me.

"You walk Varinakis here," he said. "You walk Varinakis home. Must be guarding payroll."

"I want to be sure you are both okay," I said. "I got to finish school."

Pa laughed and Mike came out of his sulk and smiled.

"What you say, big shit?" Pa said.

"Go to hell," Mike said.

"You lucky last night," Pa said and he curled his lips. "I almost kick you down few times so learn politeness to father."

"I didn't want to fight you in the middle of the night," Mike said. "Neighbors would hear you yelling for help."

Pa jeered and winked at me and then his face sobered.

"You are wild," Pa said to Mike. "You boy no more but man wild inside and that not good."

"That's fine," Mike said. "Real fine coming from Angelo Varinakis." He made a noise with his mouth. "They still tell stories about you in the bush. About the night you wrecked the Athletic Club and it took six guys to throw you out."

Pa flushed and stared down at the steel toes of his heavy shoes. "Long ago," he said. "Long time ago."

"And the night your crew set the tonnage record," I said. "I've heard men talk about that night a hundred times. How they swore the crane was a bird picking up steel like it was crumbs. How the furnaces burned like hell and the slabs came out like shells out of a cannon. About the stocker with a smashed hand who refused to leave the crew until the turn was over. Mostly about you driving the men on with a face like lightning and with thunder coming from your tongue."

Pa stood there breathing heavily, his cheeks flushed again but this time with the heat of remembering. I felt my own blood pounding suddenly in my head, seeing that night as clearly as if I had been there, thinking of myself driving the men and whipping the fury of the furnaces and the rolls so that the triumph belonged to both Pa and me.

"I remember," Pa said slowly. "I remember good."

"So what the hell do you want?" Mike asked. "I am your son. For two damn years I fight Japs. Now I got to fight you. You going to let me grow up? You want to put me back in school with Tony?"

Pa looked at me gently and nodded slowly as if to ease any hurt I might feel at being reminded I was still young and in school. He turned back to Mike with something like pleading in his eyes.

"You my son," he said. "I learn that in years you gone when I light candles and speak thousand prayers for God bring you back to home. By god, boy, I know you like I know myself. Many times men say, Angelo, that boy, Mike, he is like you. I proud, but scared too."

"Why scared, Pa?" Mike said. "Why the hell scared?"

Pa stood there and I watched his cheeks and the words that were trying to gather within his flesh. In the end, he gave up and scowled and I smiled. The scowl softened and Mike and I laughed.

"You bum sons," Pa said. "Goddam bums got no respect."

We stood there smiling at one another and then suddenly Pa spun around and gave Mike a shove that nearly tumbled him off his feet. He turned and slapped me hard across the shoulders.

"You gone nuts or something?" Mike said.

"Goddam!" Pa said. "I think about time Varinakis family throw one hell of party. Plenty dancing, plenty wine. All have big heads in morning."

"I'm ready," I said.

Mike nodded. "Me too."

Pa reached out and caught at the stocky shoulder of a mill man walking by.

"Hey, Barut," Pa said. "Angelo and bum sons going throw one damn fine party. You come?"

The mill man's eyes lit up within his unshaven and soot-darkened cheeks.

"Angelo," he said. "I'll be there! Goddam right, I'll be there."

"Bravo!" Pa said and he gave Barut a crashing slap across the back. "You see," he said to us. "Already four people for party. Family and Barut."

"Make it five," Mike said. His jaw was set hard again.

I looked quickly at Pa and for a long moment he did not speak. In the background the mill whistle shrilled and one of the men in Mike's crew on the way in yelled to him from the gate.

"All right, big shit," Pa said. "This be big party. Let girl come."

Mike turned and walked toward the gate. Pa watched him and his face was tight and dark and then he remembered me. He turned back and saw the concern I could feel on my own cheeks and in my eyes. He forced a smile and gave me another shove.

"Okay, barefoot Socrates," he said. "Walk Angelo home."

Chapter 3

In less than a week the snow was gone. The mill buildings looked black and dirty again. The air reeked of sulphur and the taste of black dust.

The snow did not melt at once. First it turned dark and the crust crumbled and in places showed bare ground. The edges melted and trickled rivulets into the gutters and ran streams into the sewers. Finally, only a patch remained here and there. Then the snow was gone.

The end of that week we threw the party. We cleared the furniture from the parlor, rolled back the rugs. We ordered a keg of beer and six gallons each of retsina and sweet red wine. Karpetsou roasted a whole young lamb and cut up blocks of mezithra cheese and baked big round loaves of crisp-crusted bread. Pa **wanted** things done right.

I felt real festive the night of the party. I guess almost

everybody did. Simonakis came thirsty and eager to dance. There was Fat Leo Baroumis and a couple of other foremen and their wives. Chris Bizakis came with his mustache black and sleek, and Barut looking like Neolithic man in a pin-stripe suit. There were a bunch of the boys from Pa's crew and many of the old Greeks from Gerontis'. There were even a few guys I was sure had not been invited, but there was plenty of wine and cheese and lamb and Pa said to hell with it.

I saw Sheila for just a moment when Mike first brought her. I said hello and felt the slim fingers of her hand in my own and looked into the deep Irish eyes. I remembered the night in Ma's room and I was ashamed. She went into the kitchen to help some of the women. A while later I saw her again with an apron about her hips and carrying a tray of cheese.

I worried a little about Pa seeing her and maybe thinking she was making herself too much at home. There were a half-dozen women carving and preparing to serve in the kitchen and maybe Pa would not notice Sheila among them. After a while, I stopped thinking about it and made up my mind to have a good time.

When Seferis brought his lyre from Arcadia, everybody clapped and cheered. We set him up on a makeshift platform in the corner of the room. When he began to play, the wild sweet wail of the mountain dances rang through the house.

"Dance!" Pa shouted and the white shirt he wore

seemed too small for his great waving arms. "Dance, patrioti!" He picked up a small table that was still in the way and almost threw it into a corner.

"I will dance or die!" Simonakis shouted, and bald and lean-boned, his long spare old body began to twist restless to be started. The whites of his eyes gleamed in the dark tight ridges of his face. A sudden clapping and stamping of feet began.

I went into the kitchen and found Sheila. "Come and watch," I said. "You've got to see this."

I pulled her back into the parlor and we stood among the men and women along the wall and watched.

Pa stood solemn in the center of the room. With a measured shuffling of his feet back and forth, he kindled the cadence of the dance. Simonakis joined him, second in the line, looking like a scarecrow beside the bull broadness of Pa. He held his handkerchief twined like a piece of rope, and Pa and he each held one end. Almost ready to begin, he raised his bald glistening head and crowed arrogantly like a bantam cock alerting the henhouse after return from a journey. Chris Bizakis joined the line, pulling by the wrists a girl in pink sandals. His white teeth gleamed under the black twirl of his mustache. Several more men and women joined the line behind him. Suddenly Pa shouted and Simonakis crowed again and Pa stamped release and the dance began.

A slow circling first and then a faster attendance as the tempo quickened. Held only by the twined handkerchief which Simonakis pulled on grimly, Pa whirled and balanced nimbly, to spin and fall on his knees and rise again with zestful grace. He slapped his heel with the palm of his hand and crouched again and spun and bounded up and a hoarse and joyous shout broke from his throat.

Behind him in the line, Simonakis danced possessed, and shook as if with fever. His ancient body, all bone and taut skin seemed like some stricken bird to want to fly. His head, back, hips, arms and fingers all trembled in some kind of frenzy reaching for the sky.

Afterwards Chris danced, agile and arrogant in his grace, pulling along the girl in pink sandals. Behind them came the shouting, tossing line of men and women.

Sheila watched the dancers with her cheeks flushed and her eyes bright. She shook her head making the soft fall of her hair tremble.

"They are wonderful," she said. "Your father is wonderful."

I felt my pride in Pa quicken and flow with the flowing of my blood.

"He is a lion," I said. "A great king lion that will never go down."

She looked at me quickly.

"Everything goes down in the end," she said. "Even the lions."

"Not Pa," I said. "Not before the mountains crumble and the oceans dry up."

62

It was true in that moment as he vigorously led the line of dancers that his strength beat in great waves across my head. I could not help but think he would go on forever.

"Who is the dark young man with the mustache?" Sheila said. "He has the spring of a cat."

A quick flame of jealousy singed my stomach.

"Chris Bizakis," I said. "A friend of Mike's."

At that moment Mike found us. His face was flushed.

"Where the hell have you been?" he said to me. "I had to bring those damn cases of wine in alone."

"I'm saving my strength," I said. I winked at Sheila.

He turned and watched the dancers. "What about Pa," he said to Sheila. "What do you think about Pa?"

"He is a lion," Sheila said and she smiled at me.

Mike laughed. "You've been talking to Tony," he said. "Tony calls him a lion."

The dance ended. The men and women in the rooms shouted and cheered and whistled until it seemed the roof of the house would be blown off. Pa stood in the center of the room, his chest heaving as he sucked in air. Simonakis bent wearily like the withered branches of an old tree. He waved his hand feebly and called for a glass of wine. The women brought him wine and he drank a glass quickly and almost at once seemed refreshed, as if the wine contained some strange elixir with the power of fresh blood.

Pa came over to where we stood. His face was still

a deep red and his hair was wet with the trickles of sweat. He barely did more than nod at Sheila. I looked at Mike and spoke quickly.

"What a show-off," I said. "Still trying to make an impression on the ladies at your age."

"You have fat head," Pa said. Between words he drew labored breath. "I dance because sons stand like rocks and I not want people say Varinakis family without blood."

Sheila listened to Pa and was smiling a little stiffly, and in sudden surprise I realized she was afraid of him.

Someone shouted for a Pentozali. Pa gave me a push.

"Now you have turn, fat head," he said.

" Come on," I said to Mike. "Let's show them something."

Mike looked from Sheila to Pa and shook his head. "I'm beat from those cases of wine," he said. "You show them."

I knew he didn't want to leave Sheila alone with Pa.

"Watch this boy," Mike said to Sheila. "Watch this boy dance."

I felt proud to be dancing the warrior's dance and started to the middle of the room. Seferis held his lyre in his lap and waited. A few of the men joined me. Chris came and handed me the end of his twined handkerchief.

"Dance, palikari," he said, and he took the place behind me in the line. "I'll hold you."

Seferis drew the short bow across the sweet-toned lyre. The line of men banded by clasped hands stood ready. I looked once more at Sheila and Mike and Pa. The dance began.

Long ago my people danced. The wild dance of priests in the sacred groves of olives. Pan dancing to strange medleys in the tangled Arcadian forests. Zeus howling as he danced upon the peaks of dark and mighty Parnassus. The bewitching dance of Ariadne of the lovely hair. Meriones at Troy who danced laughing while he fought and could not be touched by any lance.

Long ago my people danced. The shepherd fluting on the mountain before his flocks. The reveling dances in the Pythian festivals at Delphi, at the Feast of First Fruits and at the Feast of Flowers. The stern martial dances of Sparta and the laughing, living dances of Athens. The men of Leonidas dancing before Thermopylae, awaiting death and glory. The men of Alexander dancing wildly in the mountains of Macedon before crossing half the world.

The beat of the lyre quickened. I led the dance. I led the wild priests in the groves of olives. I danced laughing with Meriones at Troy and the lances missed us both. I danced with Leonidas awaiting death and glory. I danced with Alexander in the mountains of Macedon.

I danced in some kind of frenzy, goading the men behind me. I saw the weaving of the line and heard the cries and clamor as if from a thousand tongues. I broke away from Chris and bounded into the air and landed back on the floor feeling a great shout ringing from my throat.

The music stopped. I did not see him until he caught my arms but Pa was there, his own face bathed in sweat and his cheeks afire.

"Goddam, boy, no more!" he said. "You dance like crazy! Kill yourself and kill friends!"

"Jesus Christ!" Chris said and he was breathing hard. "You went nuts."

The men gathered and slapped my back. Here and there a daughter of one of the mill men waited, but I looked over their heads for Sheila. I wanted her to understand. In a way I had danced for her, to make her understand.

Pa pushed a chair into the center of the room and climbed up on it. His face was flushed with excitement and wine and he wanted to make a speech. He raised his big palmed hand for silence. Seferis played a shrill trumpeting on the lyre and everybody laughed.

"I am not good for speaking," Pa said.

"Then sit down Angelo!" some mill man shouted.

The women said *sshhhh* and Pa laughed loudly.

"I know you, Vasili!" Pa shouted back. "Come from behind wife or maybe you too drunk for stand up."

Vasili's wife stepped aside and Vasili was exposed red-faced and helpless in his chair. Everybody laughed. Pa raised his hand again.

"Welcome to Varinakis house," Pa said.

The men cheered and stamped their feet and the women clapped. Somehow Vasili shoved himself out of his chair and pushed his wife aside and stamped the loudest.

Pa waved helplessly for silence.

"By god, you sure one noisy bunch," he said. "Let Angelo finish and sit down. Feet hurt."

"Sit down now, Angelo!" Fat Leo yelled. He roared with laughter and slapped his meaty leg with his giant hand.

Pa laughed again enjoying the banter. In the corner watching Pa, Mike was laughing and Sheila was smiling.

"Who invite you?" Pa said to Fat Leo. "Be careful, maybe leave quick through biggest window in house."

Everybody laughed again and then small waspish Mrs. Pappas stepped forward.

"Angelo," she said. "You going to fall off that chair and break your fool head. Say what you got to say and sit down. The lamb is getting cold."

"Sit down now, Angelo!" Fat Leo shouted again.

Mrs. Pappas turned on him.

"You shut your face, Leo Baroumis!" she snapped.

Pa looked down at her a little shamefaced. She had taken some of his wind away.

"I only want say," he said and he was much more subdued, "welcome to house of Angelo and sons. Time now for eat plenty, drink plenty, and keep full faces off floor."

The men and women applauded and cheered and began to push to the dining room. Vasili performed a frantic little dance of pleasure and his wife pulled him along. Pa looked once more at Mrs. Pappas and closed his mouth and stepped down from the chair.

By sometime after midnight only a few of the guests who remained still stood. Fat Leo was asleep on one of the chairs, one of his great arms dangling to the floor. Vasili was just going out the door hanging desperately between his wife and his cousin from Gary. Simonakis, weary and full of wine, leaned against a radiator in the corner holding his Cretan lyre and softly strumming a melancholy mountain song to himself. Mrs. Budny and her sister, dry-skinned and unsmiling women, were trying to coax Chester into going home. Pa sat with a few remaining mill men half-heartedly arguing the ways of rolling steel.

My own head felt flushed and my stomach too full of lamb and cheese. I walked into the kitchen. Mrs. Lanaras and Mrs. Pappas were still washing dishes. Sheila was putting some of the cheese away in the icebox. A strand of taffy hair had fallen loose across her cheek pointing the weariness around her mouth.

"Where is Mike?" I asked.

"He's driving Mr. Vasili and his wife home," she said.

"You worked too hard," I said. "You worked all evening."

She didn't answer and Mrs. Lanaras handed her a tray of glasses.

"This girl is little skinny in arms," Mrs. Lanaras said, "but she knows how to work in a kitchen. Pretty too. Make some man good wife."

Sheila flushed a little and I smiled.

"Why don't you mind your own business," Mrs. Pappas said to Mrs. Lanaras. Mrs. Lanaras gave her back a haughty look.

"I have seven children," she said, looking scornfully at Mrs. Pappas' lean childless form. "Marriage is my business."

Mrs. Pappas clucked her tongue.

"It is not our fault that your husband knows only one game," she said.

Mrs. Lanaras raised her nose and muttered something to herself and stamped back to the sink.

I escaped out the back door to the porch. The night was cold and bracing to my flushed head. Above the mills the orange glow from the furnaces flickered like distant lightning across the sky.

A few moments later Mike's car drove up the alley in back of the house. The car door slammed and he walked to the house and came up the stairs. He stopped where I leaned on the railing.

"You damn fool," he said. "You going to catch pneumonia."

"It was a good party wasn't it?" I asked.

"It was okay," he said.

"Did Sheila enjoy the party?"

He stood just outside the kitchen door and the light from the transom bared his face.

"Sheila don't want parties," he said. "All she wants is for the old man to understand."

I didn't know what to say. Perhaps he expected that if he could keep bringing Sheila to the house, Pa would get to like her and change his mind. Maybe Pa's sullen indifference had showed him that was not going to work.

The kitchen door opened and a block of light fell across the porch. Sheila came out.

"I heard the car door," she said and she kissed Mike on the cheek. She turned to me. "You'll catch cold in your shirt." She said that like a sister to a younger brother and in some strange way it took root in my heart.

"I told him," Mike said. "He's got a head like a rock."

"A Varinakis head," I said.

"What lights the sky like that?" Sheila said.

"The furnaces," Mike said. "You see over there where **it's** real bright, they are tapping a heat."

We stood and watched the sky in silence and the glowing reflection of the fires trembling across the darkness.

"We burned a village on Okinawa," Mike said and his voice was low and suddenly seemed far away. "We drove the Japs out and set it on fire. The wind began to blow and we got out fast. When we were miles away the sky behind us still burned and looked like that." He stopped and shivered. "I'm cold," he said and he turned to me. "Get the hell inside will you?" He pulled at Sheila. "You're nutty as him coming out here without a coat. I'm wearing a coat and I'm cold. If you're ready I'll take you home."

She laughed impishly in the darkness.

"Mike Varinakis," she said, "defender of the faith and protector of the simple-minded. My hero."

I laughed and Mike let loose a good-humoured grunt. "I'll give you a hero across your fanny," Mike said and he pulled her close to him and she huddled in his arms.

I felt suddenly alone. It wasn't that I was jealous of Mike and Sheila but just that I felt alone. Maybe Sheila sensed that because she pulled out of his arms.

"All right, I'm ready," she said. "My coat is in the front closet. The gray one with the green scarf."

"Did you have to wear a green scarf?" I asked. "If old Simonakis sees it hanging in the closet he will choke."

They both had to laugh and Mike went in through

71

the kitchen. Sheila and I stood against the porch railing for a moment without speaking.

"Where did you learn to dance like that?" she asked.

I was glad it was dark so she would not see the pleasure that I was sure showed on my face.

"Pa taught me," I said. "He taught both Mike and me when we were just kids. Mike doesn't care much for it any more."

There was another long moment of silence.

"You're a strange boy," she said. "And this is a strange family. I think sometimes I understand Mike and then I don't know. I think you all belong someplace else, in some other age."

"Something romantic," I said. "Like Greek warriors fighting Persian invaders a couple of thousand years ago."

She moved beside me and I felt her arm brush mine. There was a funny restless stirring in my stomach.

"My ancestors were horse traders," she said. "But the Varinakis family was related to the gods. Mike told me so. He said the family coat of arms was Apollo on a jackass."

"The big lug wasn't kidding," I said.

She turned and faced me and the light from the burning sky tinted her cheeks.

"Tony, tell me something."

I felt a finger of unrest at my throat.

"Okay," I said.

"Do you think your father will ever change his mind about Mike and me?"

I took a deep breath. "I don't know," I said. "Maybe some day."

"Do you object to Mike marrying me?" Her voice was a quiet whisper and I did not answer for a moment and tried to think of the right thing to say.

"Sometimes I want you to get married to Mike," I said. "Most of the time I think I want what Pa wants, what he thinks is best for the family."

She was silent for a moment.

"I love him, Tony," she said. She said it quietly in the shadows. "I don't want to hurt you or your father. I know how Mike loves you both. But I love him too. He loves me. I need his love and I think he needs mine."

I could not help myself and suddenly shivered in the night. The way she said she loved him and needed him made me glad for Mike and yet sorry for Pa and sorry for myself and a little angry because nothing seemed to make sense.

I was grateful that Mike came back at that moment. He threw me a jacket and helped Sheila on with her coat.

"I'll go say good night to your father," she said.

"Let him alone," Mike said. "Father Kontoyannis just came and they are all hot about something."

"Good night, Tony," Sheila said.

"Good night, Sheila Cleary," I said.

"What did you two talk about?" Mike asked.

"About the gods," Sheila said. "The gods the Varinakis family are related to."

"Both of you are nuts," Mike said.

I watched them walk down the steps to the car. When I couldn't see them any longer I still heard the sharp click of Sheila's heels upon the walk.

Back in the parlor the only persons left were Pa and Simonakis standing with Father Kontoyannis. I wondered for a moment how they had managed to get Fat Leo Baroumis up and off the couch.

The priest smiled at me and reached to shake my hand.

"Tony," he said. "The party is over and you are still standing?"

"Big feet hold him to floor," Pa said. He held a leaflet of some kind in his hand and looked troubled.

Simonakis also held one of the leaflets and I took it from his hand. As I read I could feel the blood in my face. It was a crudely printed caricature of the priest mounted on a race horse and a near-naked woman astride behind him. The lettering was just as crude, bold and black; it denounced him as a libertine and gambler. Pa shook his head grimly.

"You see what animals do?" he said. "Last Sunday pass leaflets at Greek churches all over city." He finished and made a spitting sound with his mouth.

"I do not care they attack me," Father Kontoyannis said. "But if they want me out of the altar I would rather they shoot me than harm the church." He spoke softly but there was a thin and disturbed edge to his voice. "In their ignorance, they do not realize they harm others. If by blackening me they keep one troubled man from confession, or one mother and her child away from Sunday service, they blaspheme against God."

"Men who do this are sick," Pa said, and he rubbed his cheek angrily. "Tell names, Father, and we pull teeth."

Father Kontoyannis spread his hands in a gesture of helplessness. " What is the use, Angelo?" he said. "They are like the monster Hydra that Heracles sought to slay. As soon as one head is cut off, two grow in its place. In the end only by burning out the roots was the Hydra destroyed."

"The people love you, Father," Simonakis said.

"Is there only love?" the priest said softly. "Is that why some gloat over the leaflets and whisper in little groups and stop talking when I walk by. If there is only love, what feeds the suspicions and the doubts?"

Simonakis was silent.

"People will not believe," Pa said, and he held the leaflet by two fingers as if it were some kind of filth.

"People will believe," the priest said, and suddenly a great weariness was evident across his cheeks. "In their hearts they wonder and they doubt, and the help you try to give them is blunted by their doubt and your preaching is turned back in bitterness even though they do not speak."

For a moment we all stood silent, and then Pa looked down at the leaflet. He raised his head with his eyes suddenly flaming. He tore the leaflet roughly into pieces and dropped the pieces on the floor.

Father Kontoyannis smiled gently.

"You did not have to do that, Angelo," he said. "I have always known whose side you were on."

Pa looked embarrassed and coughed and then spoke quickly. "Little wine, Father," he said. "Little glass wine and piece cheese and bread?"

"A glass of wine to your health," the priest said. "Then I must go. There are Sunday services tomorrow. I know I will see you there." He turned to me. "You too, Tony."

He caught me by surprise. When we were children and Ma was alive the four of us went to church together. After she died, Pa and Mike and me kept going. When we got older Mike began to drag his heels. Pa had a couple of arguments with him and then he left him alone, except for warning him he was going to end up in hell. Pa went into such detail describing hell you would almost think he had been there at some time or other himself. Lately I had been going with him only because I didn't want him to have to sit in church alone.

But the priest must have had some special reason for wanting me there in the morning.

"I'll be there, Father," I said.

Pa brought him a glass of wine. He smiled and toasted us and drank it slowly. I brought his coat from the closet. The cuffs were worn and here and there a thread had torn loose and showed strips of lining. He slipped into the coat and stood for a moment in the doorway, a somber figure in black with the white collar around his throat.

In that moment I wondered if there was truth in the leaflet. We all stood silent and in the way he looked at us with the weariness chiseled into his face I knew he understood what each of us must be thinking. I remembered what he said to Simonakis about love, and I was ashamed.

"Good night," he said.

Pa closed the door slowly after him. He turned back to Simonakis and me.

"Long ago," he said and he spoke softly. "Mama sick and doctor give up hope. Each night priest come and sit for while beside bed. Talk of many things. Talk of ways of God and why people die. Make little easier for her and for family." He stopped and we watched him silently. His voice rose. "That priest is good man. Bastard say that priest is not good man lie in teeth and will settle with me."

Simonakis shook his head somberly.

77

"I am with you, Angelo," he said.

Pa nodded and then made a gesture of dismissal with his hands.

"One more glass wine," he said to Simonakis. "Then get hell out. Varinakis party over."

Simonakis snorted.

"You do not tell guests to leave until they are ready to go themselves," he said sharply.

Pa made a rippling noise with his mouth.

"By god," he said. "If wait for you, party go all night."

Simonakis gave him one final dirty look and went out slamming the door. Pa made a face.

"You hurt his feelings, Pa." I said.

"He be back tomorrow," Pa said. "He is still touchy because lose three games checkers last night."

"He told me he beat you last night," I said. "Who is lying?"

Pa looked at me indignantly.

"Do you believe outsider over father?" he asked. "Shame on my house."

"Okay, Pa," I said. "I give up."

We walked together once more through the hall and dining room and into the kitchen. The rooms were still a shambles. The furniture piled against the wall and napkins and wine bottles and cigar butts on the floor.

"Whose idea, this party?" Pa said.

"Angelo Varinakis," I said. "King of the bush. This party was his idea."

He looked around once more and shook his head sadly.

"By god," he said. "I sure plenty crazy."

We went up the stairs. In the hall we said good night and he paused before his room. He looked down the hall to the open door of Mike's room.

"Pa," I said quickly. "It was a great party."

He stood silent for a moment and then he smiled and made a quick nodding motion with his head.

"You said it, boy," he said. He stepped into his room and closed the door.

I did not undress at once but sat for a while by the window. The sky still burned over the fire of the furnaces. Far out in the darkness a pale moon hung above the smoke.

I felt the strangeness and wonder of the night. The same burning sky while my ma lay dying and the weary priest prayed. The burning sky and the house become so still. The shrill sweet lyre and the stamping of feet upon the floor and the dancing of wild ghosts lost in the silence of the house.

I undressed finally and climbed into bed. I shivered between the cold sheets. I shut my eyes and began thinking of kissing Sheila. I held her tightly and kissed her many times.

Chapter 4

In the morning Pa called us for breakfast. I heard his bellow breaking through my sleep and I didn't want to open my eyes and, as if he knew, Pa roared again. I remembered promising to go to church and I got wearily out of bed. In the hall I met Mike coming out of his room and we looked at each other and grunted. We walked downstairs together.

Pa stood smiling in his robe in the kitchen with the breakfast dishes set on the table and the strong coffee bubbling in the pot on the stove.

"Good morning, bum sons," Pa said, and he sounded buoyant considering the amount of wine he had consumed the night before. "Sit down and make order for breakfast. We got eggs."

"What are you so damn cheerful about?" Mike asked, and he flopped on a chair and put his head in his hands.

Pa laughed heartily and flipped a couple of pieces of toast out of the toaster on a plate.

"This morning all family go to church," he gloated, "Big shit promise priest he come too."

"All right!" Mike glared at him. "Don't blow a fuse laughing."

"Besides," Pa went on. "I had fine dream in night. I dream my sons very rich and come and say, Angelo, poor old bastard, you work too hard too long. Take trip to old country on money from us."

"First thing tomorrow, Pa," I said. "We'll buy you a pair of water wings. You can travel first class with the whales."

"Son of big heart," Pa said. "You got head like a whale."

"As long as Pa keeps his head under water he'll be okay," Mike said and there was a sting to his words.

Pa scowled at him.

"You damn right I okay," he said. "Nothing wrong with Angelo but big mouth sons."

"Pa, it's Sunday," I said. "Don't bawl us out on Sunday morning."

He turned away and lowered the heat beneath the skillet and for a few moments vigorously scrambled the eggs.

"I like mine sunnyside up," Mike said and he winked at me. That always got Pa going because he only fixed eggs the one way.

Pa looked at Mike as if he had two heads.

"Sunnyside up, sunnyside down," he said. "In one minute your damn head be sunnyside with pan on top."

I had to laugh and Mike joined in and Pa smiled. He spooned the eggs into our plates and sat down and said grace. We started to eat.

"How long you been cooking eggs, Pa?" I asked.

"Too long," he said.

"You should be improving," I said. "How come you are getting worse. These eggs are full of broken shell."

"In old country cook shell with egg," Pa said. "Good for health. Here let little piece slip in pan and loud squawk."

"Over here," Mike said, "we eat like human beings."

Pa looked at him balefully.

"You full of gas," he said sharply. "After last night maybe better you keep big mouth shut."

Mike slammed down his knife.

"Don't start that again!" he said. They sat glaring at each other.

"Listen," I said quickly. "We promised Father Kontoyannis we would get to church, so let's go. It's getting late." I looked pleadingly at Mike.

Pa stood up and he hadn't finished his eggs.

"Okay," he said and he was trying not to show he was steamed. "You both good boys. So damn good you try clean some of mess and empty bottles. Angelo shave first."

He left the kitchen and Mike and I sat in silence for a moment. I poured myself some more coffee.

"Want another cup?" I asked and he shook his head. "Pa sure makes strong coffee," I said. "It burns through the lining of your stomach."

"Yeh," Mike said. He still stared hard-faced at his plate.

"Mike," I said and I tried to keep my voice low. "Don't be so damn touchy. You don't even let Pa get the words out of his mouth before you jump."

"Then let him stay off my back," he said. The words bit from between his teeth.

I got up and turned away under a feeling of despair. They both crouched and waited as if they were animals ready to spring at the slightest provocation.

I picked up a few bottles and swept up some butts and then Pa was out of the bathroom. I went upstairs to wash and dress. Afterwards I put on a white shirt and my good blue suit. I put an extra shot of tonic on my hair and brushed it carefully.

When we were ready to leave we met in the front hall and looked one another over. Pa and Mike both wore clean white shirts and their best suits and looked very impressive.

"By god," Pa said. "This sure one beautiful family."

Even Mike had to smile.

We walked through the kitchen in single file out the back door and down to the garage. It was a bright cold morning, clear for November, and only a few traces of misty clouds scattered across the sky. But the ground was winter cold and hard beneath our feet.

As Mike backed the car out of the garage, Simonakis in a black suit that made him look like a long-legged undertaker came running disjointedly across the alley.

"Do not leave without me," he shouted.

Pa waved impatiently.

"Hurry up," he said. "If you not stay so late at parties maybe you be ready in morning on time."

Simonakis gave him a dirty look.

"I am riding with you to church," he said. "I do not have to talk to you."

Pa shrugged.

"My good luck," he said.

We drove to church. On the way in we met several mill men and their wives who had been to the party the night before. They were subdued in their greetings and we walked into church together.

We paused in the narthex connecting the outside with the inner church to light candles and kiss the holy ikon. We walked up one of the aisles and found places to sit together.

When I was a child and went to church with Mike and Pa, I found it a place of strange magic. I felt myself ringed and in a way sanctified within the mosaics of Christ and the Cross, and the ikons of the fierce-eyed and lonely saints beneath the flickering of hundreds of candles. On the ceiling of the church had been painted a massive figure with burning eyes, white-haired and white-bearded in wild swirling robes. God, the Pantokrator. His great hand extended toward the benches below, and when I looked up, a long finger pointed like the gun of judgment at my head. I used to wonder whether that angry and vengeful manifestation could be God. When I grew older I heard the old Greeks in the coffeehouse say the ceiling had been painted long ago by an unfrocked priest who had later gone mad. For a long time the terrible vision of it rode my dreams.

The services had started a short time before and Father Kontoyannis in bright vestments chanted before the altar. The long thin choirmaster in a shapeless black gown raised his hand and the deep ringing tones of the organ pealed across the church. The voices of the choir sang the rich and melancholy Byzantine hymns. The incense burned and drew trails of smoke upon the solemn church.

Pa watched and listened intently and moved his lips with the prayers. Mike sat bored, and fidgeting already. Beside him Simonakis sat hunched with his bald head glistening in the mist of the candles.

I thought our mass too long and our ritual too involved. Several times on Sundays, without telling Pa or Mike, I had visited other churches trying to relate the act of faith and worship to our own. I heard simple services of sometimes moving beauty. Coming out into daylight afterward I envied in a way their uncluttered relationship with God. But in the end, with whatever allegiance I could muster, I came back to the church of my father. For when you have been raised among candles and incense and the melancholy hymns, when you have looked up as a child and trembled beneath the eye and finger of God pointing like judgment at your head, it is not easy to turn to simpler faiths.

The congregation had risen. Father Kontoyannis brought out the chalice of communion and held it above his head. The altar boys with freshly-scrubbed cheeks held the long-stemmed candles. The choir raised their voices again and the organ tones echoed about our heads.

Later in the quiet church with the organ at rest, Father Kontoyannis stood before us and began to speak.

"I will speak today of myself," he said. "Of what it means to be a minister in our faith. How I began and what road I traveled to finally raise the chalice and speak to you of God."

He spoke calmly and in a resonant voice and his cheeks were pale above the bright vestments.

"Some might find their faith with ease," he said. "I cannot say how it is for them. But I came to the church after much searching in my heart. I came slowly, and many times I stopped and thought of turning back. I saw no great light such as was visited upon Paul on the road to Damascus. My nights were long and filled with anguish, and uncertainty carried into my days."

I sat still and listened. A deep and heavy silence had fallen across the church and only an occasional cough could be heard as he paused a moment between words.

"My father had been a priest before me. It was his prayer that I follow in his ways. He spoke to me often of the glory of serving God. He was a man with a vision that burned in him like a flame and gave me warmth. In some mystical way I thought I could become another man. I would be one of the chosen of God and his light and gratitude would shine upon me."

From a rear bench a baby wailed a thin faraway cry. The candles burned and trailed wisps of smoke about the altar. His voice, rising slowly, bound us together.

"I prayed for four years in the monastery. I studied my catechism until I knew the text by heart. I waited for a sign that God was aware of my zeal. That he would unravel for me the mystery of suffering — the antagonism at the heart of the world. I could not say, 'Thy will be done,' about the suffering of the innocent. I could not accept the sins of the fathers visited upon the sons. I could not believe that God could be merciful and permit children to be lame and blind, and young women to die in childbirth and the sick to cry out in pain. But the terrible grace of God's truth was denied to me. Until one day I woke with terror to the knowledge I would soon have to speak of God to other men."

His hand rose and fumbled at the collar of his vestment. His fingers gripped the cloth and then moved again as if in search of a place to rest. I felt my breath catch sharply in my own throat. He looked to the ceiling and a multitude of faces turned silently upward and the finger of God pointed to us all.

"I was also in terror of turning back. I lacked the courage to forsake the years of prayer and the vision of my father's faith. I comforted myself that if God were merciful someday I must be granted understanding. I accepted my ordainment knowing it meant I could never marry."

His hands no longer moved restless and searching, but knotted together firmly against his chest. He raised his head and the candles flickered and burned across his cheeks.

"Now I have been a priest for almost thirty years, twenty-six years in this parish. I tell you now what I have learned in that time. I am only a man. Strip off my robes and you will find my flesh as vulnerable as your own. In the winter I am cold as you are cold. In the summer nights I lie restless with the heat and cannot sleep. If I go long without food I hunger. If I do not drink water I thirst." His voice rose slightly and seemed to swell and gather force. "If at times your bones ache and you wish to lie longer in bed on Sunday morning, know that I feel this ache too. If at times you are weary of the endless ritual of the mass, know that I have felt this weariness too. If at times you are caught in selfishness or greed or lust, know that your thought is no worse than my own."

The baby wailed again, and closer suddenly an old woman began to cry. A restless whisper of voices hissed across the church. The priest stepped forward and raised his hand. His voice rang out loud and clear as the striking of a great bell.

"I would that I might stand before you and say I am without the weaknesses of men. I cannot. I am a man and my life is struggle. I know I will struggle till I die."

Pa sat pale and hanging on each word. Mike listened with his big hands squeezed between his knees. Simonakis sat straight up with stiff back and tense head. The faces of the men and women around us were caught in some bright and sudden light. They looked uneasily at one another. The priest raised his hands again for silence. The sleeves of his vestments fell back and his wrists sprang like pale stalks from within the folds of cloth. His voice rang above the hum and hiss that raced through the church.

"If you can bear with me and help me and let me help you, we may go on together. If you are beggars, know me as a beggar who prays beside you. If you are sick, I know your pain because it is my own. I know your wandering in darkness because the path is mine as well. Help me. Let me help you. Perhaps in that way we will draw nearer to God together."

89

He finished and bowed his head. The vestments across his shoulders rose and fell as if he was breathing deeply. The church held silent for a long moment and then a single angry curse ripped harshly from some man's mouth. A hundred heads twisted and scores of men and women rose and Pa rose and clenched his fists and looked furiously around. A few voices cried shame and through it all the priest stood unmoving. The whispers started again, as men and women sat down, flashing across the church as fire through dry brush.

Pa sat down and the tears were naked and unashamed upon his cheeks. I had not seen Pa cry since Ma died and that I only remembered faintly, but this was real and I felt it beat into my own flesh. Mike was staring at Pa, too, his cheeks loose and unmoving.

The organ sounded again, strange and resonant across the unquiet church.

" Glory to thee, O our God," the choirmaster sang and his voice sounded a little strained. Father Konto-yannis turned to the altar and raised his hands. His deep rich voice rose winged above our heads.

"Blessed be the Kingdom of the Father and of the Son and of the Holy Ghost, now and forever, and from all ages to all ages."

"Amen," the choirmaster said.

The services were over. The girls of the choir in black robes with white collars formed in a single line and passed the altar and received the small pieces of bread from the hand of the priest. The men and women in the church rose and some went to the altar to accept the bread, and others hung back in small whispering groups, and still others muttered angrily and did not care who heard.

"I go for bread," Pa said.

Mike and I walked with him to take our places in line. Simonakis hurried to get in line before us.

Mike nudged me with his elbow and grinned.

"He really bombed the place," Mike said and he was pleased. "He sent them all to hell."

"It wasn't like that," I said and even as I spoke I was trying to understand. I could still hear his words ringing through the silent church and see the pale nakedness of his face beside the waning candles.

"What was it like then?" Mike asked. "I say he sent them all to hell where most of them deserve to go."

"It just wasn't like that," I said. "He wasn't speaking in arrogance. He told them the way it was with him. I think he was saying that we are all men, that he is no more than a man, that we cannot expect any more than that."

"It took guts," Mike said. "I got to admit what he did took guts."

Yes, that much was clear. What he had done took guts, a rare and mighty courage.

When our turn came to receive bread from his hand I looked for some sign of the ordeal on his face, but his eyes were masked and his cheeks impassive. Only when I accepted my piece of bread and slowly bent and kissed the back of his hand did I feel the fingers moist and trembling slightly.

We waited to the side of the church until he had dispensed the last pieces of bread. Then he turned and passed beside the altar to the hidden rooms beyond.

"What are we waiting for, Pa?" Mike asked.

"We see priest," Pa said and he shook his head slowly. "I find hard understand why he speak. Why?"

"Pa," I said. "Pa, it was a great thing. . . ." Then I stopped. The sexton passed us and began to snuff out the candles along the walls and across the front of the church. The ikons of the saints were cloaked in a rapidly darkening mist. I looked up to the dome and the painted God was all but obscured. I could not help myself and shivered.

A man came up the aisle from the rear of the church and I recognized the quick disjointed walk of Simonakis. When he reached us he was breathing hard.

"There is anger outside," he said. "Men and women who feel the church has been defiled. They wait for the priest." He paused for a moment to catch his breath, his leathery cheeks trembling. "I do not like it, Angelo," he said. "His friends have gone and the ones against him have stayed."

"Priest will not be harmed," Pa said and the way he

spoke with iron in his voice stirred a sudden violence in my stomach.

The church was almost completely dark by then and Pa tugged at my arm.

"Wait here," he said to Mike and Simonakis. "Tony, come with me inside."

I followed him around the benches of the choir and we walked slowly because we could not clearly see our way. Before the small door of the room beside the altar that had the panels decorated with a painting of St. George slaying the dragon, Pa stopped and knocked.

A moment of silence and then a partly muffled voice called to us to come in.

We entered into a small dimly lit room heavy with the scents of oil and incense. Father Kontoyannis, still in his vestments, stood before a symbol of the crucifixion and even as he turned to us I knew he had been praying. His lips were tightly closed and his face was masked within the shadows of the room.

"Father," Pa said, and he paused and seemed to be trying to find the right words. "Father," and then he stopped and stood silent.

The priest turned and began unhooking the cords that bound the layers of his vestments.

"Angelo," he said. "Angelo, we have known each other so many years. I understand what you want to say." He turned to me. "Tony, please help me with my vestments." I moved quickly and stepped close to him and my fingers fumbled at the knotted cords. I could sense an agitation in his body and in a way it struck disorder into my flesh.

"Father," Pa said. "Some of people are angry."

"I know," the priest said. "I know."

"We walk with you," Pa said.

The priest's eyes flashed and he stiffly shook his head.

"I need no bodyguard," he said. "If I must be protected leaving my church it is time I leave for good."

"People are angry," Pa said and he clenched his fists. "Angry fools do foolish things."

"They will not harm me," the priest said and for the first time since we entered the room he loosened his mouth in a grim smile. "Perhaps they will curse me a little and bite at me with their eyes but they will not harm me. That takes a courage most of them do not have."

Pa stared at him for a long moment and then unclenched his fists and let his hands hang helplessly by his sides.

"Father," he said, and the word came with effort from his mouth. "You say today you are man like me." He stopped and shook his head in wonder. "I do not understand."

The priest stepped away from me and raised his arms above his head. I saw his frail wrists and the long pale fingers, and I remembered again the moment of his

94

revelation and the restless movement of his hands. He bent forward and I tugged the heavy brocaded vestment off over his head. When he straightened up, his white hair was mussed.

"Angelo," he said quietly. "I am a man like you. You have to understand that."

Pa shook his head.

"You are priest," he said and his words fell like hammers. "You teacher of word of God. You are more than man."

"Angelo, Angelo . . ." Father Kontoyannis said and there was pain open and sharp across his cheeks.

"Why you not say rumors lie?" Pa burst out. "Why you not say pigs spit lies?"

"What if they did not lie?" the priest said and he spoke in distress and looked straight at Pa. "What if there was some truth in what they spit? What would you have me say to them?" Pa listened with his face naked and unbelieving. The whisper of the priest's voice sharpened and his eyes gleamed in the weary circles of his face. "Angelo, what is uglier than a hypocrite? To listen to confession and have a man humble before you and know within yourself that you are the same. What if I denied and fought the rumors and tried to separate the small truths from the great black lies." He paused and moved his head in some shaken violence. "I am not asking absolution because most of what they say is untrue. It matters little that I am an old man

95

with small taste for extravagant debauchery. A meager sin to escape dark loneliness is still a sin and must be paid for in the end. So I have told them all my feet are clay. The arrogant ones and the righteous ones and those poor Christians that wear their respectability like a coat of armor, they will bite at me behind my back and cross the city to another church and perhaps even petition the bishop to expel me. I am not concerned with them. They sit in church like it is their house and God is the intruder. But the others, Angelo, the sick and the troubled and the driven. Now that I have discarded the mask of the hypocrite perhaps they will come to me more freely. We can pray together. Perhaps I can better serve God in this way."

When the priest finished, Pa and I stood in silence. I tried hard to separate what I felt at that moment. Compassion for him and awe before his courage.

"You crazy man, Father," Pa said, and he spoke softly. "They will hang you on cross and drive in long nails. You better man than all of us, but you crazy too."

The priest smiled gently.

"Angelo, you hurt for me. It makes you angry that some will think badly of me. You rise to defend me even against myself as you would rise to defend your sons. Thank you, my friend, but do not despair. I may have to carry the cross on my back, but I do not think they will crucify me on it."

Pa looked down and the priest turned to me. He stood in his shirtsleeves and from a shelf took down the small bib of black cloth with the stiff white collar attached. He put the collar around his throat and fumbled behind his neck for the button. He reached for his suitcoat and I took it and held it for him. He pulled down the cuffs of his shirt and held them in his fingers so they would not hike up. He motioned with his wrists.

"Tony, do you see these studs?" he said and they were square and white with the image of a church carved delicately upon the surface which was bone or ivory. "In the old country they belonged to my father. On Sunday morning, I would put them in his shirt. I would help him on and off with his vestments as you helped me now." He paused and looked toward the crucifix on the wall. "I will never forget that church," he said. "It stood at the foot of Lania, the mountain of many sheep. There was one stained-glass window above and behind the altar. In the early morning the sun would shine upon the altar and my father in his vestments. The whole church would glimmer with the soft and golden colors of light."

He gripped the cuffs again and turned his back. I slipped his coat over his arms. For a moment my face was close to his.

"Tony," he said, and spoke quietly in almost a whisper. "Do you understand?"

"I think I understand, Father," I said.

He nodded and seemed pleased. He turned to Pa, who had not moved.

"Come, Angelo," he said. "It is getting late and I have promised to take lunch with Niko Carabasos and his family." He smiled a little ruefully. "I do not know whether the invitation is now withdrawn, but we will see."

He pushed open the swinging door and Pa and I followed. In the church he seemed to brace his shoulders and then walked firmly and erectly down the center aisle.

Simonakis and Mike waited for us beside the organ.

"He should not walk out alone," Simonakis said in agitation. "Some people are angry. They will stone him."

"Let the bastards try," Mike said. He started after the priest.

"No," Pa said quietly.

"You going to let him walk out alone?" Mike asked angrily.

"Let him alone," I said. "Mike, he didn't want us with him."

The priest passed through the narthex in the rear of the church and for a brief moment was revealed, a small dark figure against a block of daylight as he opened the door, and then we were locked again in the silence and the dark.

I tried to make out Pa's face almost lost in heavy

shadows. None of us spoke. Then Pa walked quickly toward the door and we followed.

In the narthex Pa pushed open the door and the daylight was bright and made me blink. There were several small groups of men and women, dark faced and hostile, silently watching the priest. He had reached the base of the stairs, still erect, and on the last step a heavy-shouldered man spit at his feet. The priest faltered for just a moment but did not turn his head and kept walking.

Pa's face was suddenly flame and fury and he went quickly down the stairs and stopped before the big man who had spit. Mike moved closer and I followed and recognized the man as a butcher with a shop on Dart Street, a heavy-armed man who split chops and sliced the rolls of meat.

"What do you want?" the butcher asked Pa and he had a harsh and angry voice.

Then Pa hit him. It was a tremendous blow delivered in fury and indignation and with all the force of Pa's hand and massive shoulder. It caught the butcher in the face with a sound of a cleaver striking the block, and shot him backwards against the short railing. For a desperate moment, with his senses rattled, he struggled for support. Then a twisting shudder relaxed his body and he fell back and his feet swept off the ground and he tumbled over the railing to the ground.

Pa looked furiously around, but no man or woman moved or spoke in the butcher's defense. From somewhere in the distance the sounds of the city could be faintly heard, but we waited in a long silence.

Pa moved then and walked defiantly off the stairs and Mike and Simonakis and I followed. I was suddenly conscious of my heart pounding and my tongue dry in my mouth.

I looked once at the stricken butcher crumpled on the ground, and for a terrible moment I was afraid he might be dead. Then he stirred slightly and moved his lips without making a sound and tried to move his limbs.

We walked to the car and Simonakis chuckled under his breath and Mike gave me a broad wink. Even Pa seemed a little less troubled and walked briskly without looking back.

Chapter 5

THE CLASS SAT RESTLESS AND STIRRED IN ANTICIPA-
tion. Beside his desk on the lecture platform, short, dark-
browed Dr. Kamratt watched us from behind horn-
rimmed glasses. He stood holding the questions to be
distributed for our examination in Philosophy 201.

In the chair next to mine, burly Charley Little in his
varsity sweater appeared already in pain. On the other
side of me, Dennis Ahearn, who always wore a shirt and
tie to class and whose grandfather had been in prison
with Parnell, was chewing the eraser on his pencil. In
front of Dennis, pretty Sarah Fallon had her green plaid
skirt pulled an inch above her knees while she scratched
her leg. Sarah had long and graceful legs which I
ardently admired. The rest of the class, an assortment of
heads and hunched backs, sat waiting.

"In moments of meditation," Dr. Kamratt said, "I am possessed by admiration at my courage." He placed his fingers across his nose and let a slight grim trace of smile peep through. "How can any man without abundant courage teach philosophy to the youth of today? How can any man without bountiful stamina speak of justice and truth and morality before cynical and unimpressed young heads? But in fairness, mention should be made as well of your courage in taking this course. Now, on the eve of Christmas vacation, faced with conquering your first term examination before two weeks of freedom, I salute you."

Dr. Kamratt did indeed salute us, waving his lean-fingered hand in a wide sweep that included all the room.

"I will not give credence to those despoilers," he said, "who suggest my class is composed of refugees from physiological psychology that meets at this same time. That after earnest deliberation of the classes available at this hour, mine was selected as the lesser of a number of evils. No, I would rather believe that a sincere desire for small truths and a genuine love of wisdom brought you here. Mr. Little, is this not so?"

Mr. Little looked startled. The class was silent out of pity for Mr. Little.

"Yes sir," Mr. Little said, painfully.

"Good," Dr. Kamratt said and he nodded his head in

sardonic approval. "Mr. Ahearn, is that also the reason you took this course?"

Mr. Ahearn, with all the dignity one would expect in a young man whose grandfather had been in prison with Parnell, answered without hesitation.

"Yes sir," Mr. Ahearn said.

I had to smile.

"Mr. Varinakis is smiling," Dr. Kamratt said. "A great smile of confidence. Or is it perhaps arrogance? He is secure in his knowledge that he plans to be a teacher and that he is a descendant of Plato and Aristotle. In some strange and secret stirring of blood he has what the rest of us must struggle so hard to acquire. Is that right, Mr. Varinakis?"

I flushed a little. Sarah Fallon giggled and Dennis Ahearn smirked. I glared at them both.

"No sir," I said.

Dr. Kamratt shook his head dolefully.

"I am pleased you are aware of that, Mr. Varinakis," he said. "Customs change. Blood is not enough. Socrates was given poison for what was then called corruption of the minds and morals of the young. This was of course long before the cultural advent of television. I am quite sure, had the revered teacher lived today, he might have finished up a contestant on some quiz program. Therefore, it is probably just as well that in his own time he managed to die with dignity surrounded by a few grieving friends who loved him. You will all remember in one of our earlier sessions how beautifully Plato describes the death of Socrates in the *Apology*. Do you remember, Mr. Varinakis?"

"Yes sir," I said.

"Good," Dr. Kamratt said. He looked silently for a long moment at the class and then audibly sighed.

"If after three or nine months in this class," he said, "you can at least carry away the memory of the dignity of Socrates upon the day of his execution, your time here will not have been spent in vain. If at some later stage in your life, as gladiators in the arena of commerce, or as harried fathers and mothers faced with the insurrection of obstinate sons, you remember the dignity and wisdom of that bald, round-faced teacher who asked gently of everything, of justice and truth and virtue and morality, *'ti einai* — what is it?' I will be more than pleased, I will be profoundly grateful. Can you understand that, Mr. Varinakis?"

As he spoke I was conscious of an intensity within his words behind the barb and the jest and the disappointments that he wore as if they were the fabric of an old coat no longer able to conceal abuse. For a disquieting moment he stood revealed as vulnerable. So that for an apprehensive instant it seemed to me I understood something of what it meant to be a teacher.

"Yes sir," I said.

Dr. Kamratt nodded with finality.

"Then let us begin. It is now a few moments past one o'clock. You will have approximately two hours to complete the examination. Are there any questions?"

There were no questions.

Dr. Kamratt distributed the papers. Charley Little bent his big shoulders forward despondently. Dennis Ahearn stopped chewing the eraser on his pencil. Sarah Fallon pulled her skirt far down over her fine knees.

A pained silence fell over Philosophy 201.

I came home from school that last afternoon with nothing to worry about over the Christmas holidays but the results of my exams and working extra hours at Rothstein's store. I came into the house the back way, slamming the kitchen door. I walked into the hall off the dining room and threw my books on a chair. That's when I saw them in the parlor.

I noticed the girl first because she was sitting by the window in Pa's chair, the one he read his evening paper in. The pale afternoon sun through the lace curtains fell like a mantilla across her head. She appeared lost in the big chair and seemed only a child until I looked more closely and realized she was near my own age.

She was black-haired with her hair chopped so short it seemed carved about her head. Her eyes watching me gleamed dark and big above the milkiness of her cheeks. Her neck was long and slender and appeared much too fragile to carry her fierce little head.

The other woman in the room sitting on the couch cleared her throat. She was heavy and many-chinned with a wide flushed face and frozen eyes. She wore a hat with a floppy brim and an absurd bird on the crown. Upon the straining cloth dress that covered her ample breasts, a great brooch gleamed like the eye of Cyclops.

"You are Tony," the woman said, and she smiled beneath the floppy brim and showed big glittering teeth. "Of course, did not your Papa tell of our visit?"

Then I remembered Mrs. Bratsos and her daughter from Albuquerque. Mr. Bratsos and Pa had been close friends in the old country and had emigrated to America together. As a child, once, after Ma died, I had visited them for a few weeks with Pa. They lived in a small stucco house at the edge of the city and in the morning, the mountains towered snow-capped in the distance. I had played with this girl in Albuquerque. Studying for my exams, I had forgotten Pa telling me of their visit.

"Sure," I said. "I'm sorry I busted in the way I did." I smiled in apology at the girl.

"You have become quite a tall young man," Mrs. Bratsos said and her voice was quick and shrill. "You resemble your poor mama, her deep eyes and high forehead. You mama was fairer than your papa, not so dark."

I kept looking from her to the girl, smiling foolishly, I was sure, at both of them.

"Your papa went down the street," Mrs. Bratsos said, "to send a telegram to Mr. Bratsos that we arrived well. Mr. Bratsos has not been well. Not well at all."

I tried to appear sympathetic and stared again at the girl. Mrs. Bratsos cleared her throat sharply.

"You remember Marika?" she asked. "Of course you must remember Marika. Marika, this is Tony. You remember Tony?"

In Albuquerque I remembered Marika as a slim, dark-haired little girl with big sad eyes and a rag doll she would never let out of her arms. We tried to play together but always ended up in a fight. Once she asked me where my mother was and I told her she had gone on a long trip. Marika looked at me out of those knowing eyes and told me my mother was dead and explained without faltering what being dead meant.

I didn't care much then for Marika or her mother. As for Mr. Bratsos, I remembered him as small and insignificant beside the broad strength of Pa. A man who moved like a shadow among the celery and cabbages in his narrow store. But a kind man, too, who had a gentle smile and gave me clusters of shiny grapes and ripe dark plums.

The kitchen door slammed again and a moment later Pa came into the parlor.

"Good you home," he said to me and slapped my shoulder. "You remember Marika and Aunt Stella? You remember Aunt Stella and Uncle George?"

107

"Sure, Pa," I said. "I remember." We had called each other's parents aunt and uncle although we were not really related.

"Tony in senior year in college," Pa said proudly. "When he puts hard head down, makes fine marks."

All this time the girl sat there not saying a word, her hands clasped in her lap. While Pa spoke she watched him steadily.

"Marika finished high school in Albuquerque," Mrs. Bratsos said. "Then one year in junior college with all subjects A. George and I wished to send her to college." She shrugged her fleshy shoulders and it wiggled the brooch on her breast. "But the way things are," she said, "George sick and the store making almost nothing."

Pa shook his head, concern for his friend mirrored on his cheeks.

"Angelo, if you knew," Mrs. Bratsos said in her shrill voice, "what I have to put up with and what I have been through. George in and out of the hospital and my trying to keep house and manage the store too." She paused a moment for breath and remembered Marika. "Of course Marika helps all she can, but the real burden is on me."

Marika stared at her fingers in her lap.

"Is too bad George sick," Pa said. "That man work too hard for many years."

Mrs. Bratsos shook her head in a quick heaving of her chins.

"George works hard," she said, "but I help him all I can. I cook at home. I go to the store. If you knew what I have to go through."

Pa smiled gently at Marika.

"Maybe you tired from long trip," he said. "Maybe rest for little while." He motioned to the suitcases beside the couch. "Tony take cases upstairs and show you Mama's room where you sleep."

"Ma's room?" I asked surprised.

Pa understood and silently shook his head as if to ask where else could the two women sleep?

Marika stood up and she wore a plain gray jersey dress that sheathed her slim body and pinched her delicate waist. I looked cautiously at her breasts and they were small and only slightly outlined against her dress. Somehow that made me sorry for her.

I picked up the suitcases and waited for her in the doorway to the hall.

"I'll carry the smaller one," Marika said, and those were the first words she had spoken since I entered the room. Her voice was soft and pleasing and unlike her mother's.

"They're not heavy," I said.

"Let big shot show off muscles," Pa said.

I gave him a dirty look and stood holding the suitcases and feeling foolish again. Marika gave me a faint smile and started up the stairs and I followed.

She had the most astonishingly attractive behind rising in small and perfectly matched half-moons from the long slenderness of her legs. I was sure she wasn't wearing a girdle. She did not wiggle when she walked as some girls do, but the flesh did bob up and down in a disquieting rhythm. I imagined what she would look like in brief shorts or a bathing suit and felt a warm tightness knotting in my body. I hoped desperately she wouldn't turn around for fear something of what I was thinking might show on my face.

In Ma's room I put down the suitcases and switched on the light. She came just inside the door and stopped and I watched her face.

"It's a sad room," she said finally, and there were tears somewhere just behind her eyes.

I felt strange at the way she said that.

"Why is it sad?" I asked. "We never think of it as a sad room. It was Ma's room and she is dead and these are her things."

She shook her head slowly and her mouth trembled slightly.

"It is sad because she is dead," she said, "and left all these things to sit unused in a lonely room. It is sad because where she is she has nothing."

I watched her dark and brooding eyes. In a way she was right, and a chill touched my back and I thought of Ma alone in the cold and uncaring earth.

"I'm sorry," she said suddenly. "I should not have said that."

"Never mind," I said. I picked up the suitcases and stood holding them uselessly. She made me feel so uneasy.

"I remember you," she said and she spoke without smiling. "You stole grapes from me, and once you pushed me off my bicycle and made me cry."

"It's been years," I said. "I wouldn't push you off your bicycle now." I put the suitcases back on the floor.

She turned away and the back of her neck gleamed pale and looked strangely warm. She fingered the fringe of lace on the canopy of the bed.

"These things won't be unused forever," I said. "When Mike and I marry, Pa will give them to our wives." I was conscious of my voice as she turned and felt my cheeks flushed.

She didn't speak but turned her back again and I moved and bumped the damn suitcases. I picked them up and walked to the wall and set them down hard.

"I'm off for Christmas vacation," I said. "I'll take you downtown while you're here if you like."

She didn't seem to be listening but moved slowly around the room before the old country dishes and crystal.

Suddenly I felt angry.

"You don't talk very much, do you?" I asked sharply.

She stopped then and turned on me with those big dark eyes.

"Does that bother you?"

"I think it does," I said. "I'm struggling to keep a conversation going to be polite and you leave me high and dry."

Her dark eyes flashed.

"Don't struggle to keep talking for my sake."

"All right, I won't."

"All right, don't."

She stood there slim and furious. She didn't remind me at all of Angela with the mouth ripe as a plum or Sarah Fallon with the dimpled knees or even Sheila Cleary. I had never known a girl quite like her before. Then I reminded myself she was a guest in our house.

"I'm sorry," I said.

"Being sorry doesn't excuse bad manners."

That took my breath away.

"What bad manners?" I asked. "The only thing I did was mention you didn't talk very much."

"You must be used to girls that talk all the time," she said. "Silly girls that do nothing but giggle and chatter."

There was something wrong with this girl.

"I understand now," I said.

She gave me a long stern look.

"Understand what?"

"Why I pushed you off your bicycle in Albuquerque."

She tossed her head and pushed up the dark short single curl that fell across her forehead. There was almost a trace of a smile somewhere on her face.

"What are you studying in school?" she asked.

"History, philosophy, sociology," I said. "I want to teach."

"I wanted to go on in school," she said, "but a girl doesn't need an education to get married." The words were sullen off her tongue.

"Are you engaged back home?" I asked. She didn't answer for a moment, her cheeks pointed with some deeper bitterness.

"In Albuquerque there are mountains and Indians," she said, "and I'm not engaged to anybody."

She said things in such a crazy way, in a way that seemed to cut the conversation short and leave me nothing to add. I stood there watching her and suddenly remembering things the last few weeks. Pa telling me that Mrs. Bratsos and Marika would be coming for a few days before Christmas. Several times after that a man or woman at our house sitting with Pa in the parlor in whispered conversation. They always stopped talking when I passed through the hall.

The crazy puzzle fell into place. This slim dark girl from the mountain city had come for a husband. That explained the visit for just a few days and the whispered conversations in the parlor. That did not explain her bitterness or how quickly she could be stung to anger, unless she had come unwillingly, and that made no sense at all. Nobody could force her into a marriage she did not want. At least I didn't think that was possible.

I knew in an inbred community such as ours, marriages were arranged all the time. Just a few months before there had been the nephew of Mrs. Boukamas brought from Greece for the eldest daughter of Andrew Kaferakis, and the engagement contract made before they met.

Pa laughed when I argued with him against this. He had assisted in several compacts himself and always believed the arrangements were made with the best interest of the parties in mind. A dinner perhaps at which the man and girl were given an opportunity to meet each other and members of their families. Afterwards only if both were willing to proceed were further plans developed.

Except that sometimes the men were on the far side of fifty with an uneasy taste for a young girl.

Marika watched me defiantly as if she knew what I had been thinking.

"It's been a long time," she said, "since Albuquerque."

Her ma's voice shrilled up the stairs.

"Your ma is calling," I said and at that moment I was glad.

"I heard her," she said. She turned to leave.

There was something else I wanted to say but couldn't find the right words then.

"Listen," I said. "I go to work now but I'll see you tonight."

She stopped in the doorway and watched me silently for a moment and then nodded and left the room.

In a few moments I followed her downstairs. She was in the kitchen with her mother and Pa.

"I got to go to the store, Pa," I said. "I'll be back about ten." I gave him a hard, accusing look.

"Maybe we be gone tonight," Pa said. He was busy with a pan near the stove and did not notice my stare. "I switch turn with Fat Leo and maybe with Aunt Stella and Marika we visit friends. Supper for you and Mike on top of stove."

Marika was standing beside the kitchen table and did not look up. I said good-by and went out the back door.

When I returned home that night sometime after ten the house was empty. Mike wouldn't be home from his shift at the mill until after midnight. Pa had left breaded chops wrapped in foil on the stove and sliced tomatoes and cheese in the icebox.

I ate something and sat for a while in the kitchen. I couldn't get it out of my head. Marika coming all the way from Albuquerque to contract marriage with some man she had not yet met.

The dampness and cold seemed to have seeped into the house and through my bones. I went upstairs to the bathroom to brush my teeth and undress. There were silk stockings hanging on the rack, sheer and fit for slender legs. I touched them and felt a quivering in my stomach.

In my bed the sheets were cold and the room smelled of raw winter. A window frame was loose and every few moments, under a disturbing wind, it made a sound as if castanets were being shaken sharply.

I was tired of going to bed alone. Almost twenty-one years on earth without a single jump. All the damn girls in the city, all the lovely warm-bodied girls rolling in countless beds with other men.

Suddenly I was angry at Pa who indifferently provided bed companions for girls who came from Albuquerque, and angry at girls who allowed themselves to be sold, and angry at those boastful cocksmiths in college who notched conquests on their belts.

Damn me for a virgin and a fool.

There was the jarring of a car door in the front of the house and a scatter of good nights, among them Pa's deep voice. In a moment they came into the house.

I listened for a while to the muffled voices rising through the floor from the kitchen. Every so often the swelling of the wind shook the frame and drowned them out.

I must have fallen asleep for a while, but not long, because in waking I still heard the voices downstairs. There had been a brief and disordered dream I could not remember, but my body felt flushed and tight.

I left my bed and went quietly down the hall to the

bathroom. Pa's voice came clearly from the kitchen and he was talking of the old days and Ma. I touched the knob of the bathroom door and heard the water running. I knew suddenly it must be Marika. I moved to return to my room and the door opened.

She stopped abruptly as if I had startled her. The small light at the end of the hall cut strips of shadows across her eyes and mouth. She wore shiny soft-looking pajamas and her feet on the floor were small and bare. We stood there for a moment without moving, close enough for me to smell the fresh scents of soap and talcum, and see the naked, pale hollow of her throat.

I was suddenly conscious of my flushed body, and something born of anger and the dream cried out in me at how near she was and how silent under shadow. She moved then to pass me and I blocked her path and caught her arm. I was scared but frenzied too in a way that would not let me stop and I pulled her against me and felt the soft nipples of her breasts and the slight teasing of her breath across my cheek.

I kissed her and for just a moment felt the fullness of her lips smelling of some sweet sharp toothpaste.

Then in sudden panic I let her go and she twisted quickly and padded on bare feet toward her room, the cloth of the pajamas moving easily about her thighs. She went into the room without looking back and closed the door quietly.

Back in my room I climbed under the covers really shaking and my heart beating like crazy. I thought of what Pa or her ma would have said if they had seen. But mostly I twisted hot and remembered Marika, the way her body felt in my arms, the softness of her breasts and the toothpaste sweetness of her lips.

I was scared she might tell, and surprised at myself and glad, too. In a way a little hard to understand I was glad.

In the morning I woke early, in cold clear daylight, remembering what I had done. I must have been crazy and couldn't even remember whether she had kissed me back. The prospect of facing her unnerved me, and then all I could think of was getting dressed and out of the house.

I dressed quickly and went quietly downstairs, into the smell of fresh coffee from the kitchen. I considered slipping out the front door, but Pa heard me and came into the hall.

"Good morning, youngest son," he said. "You up early."

Then I couldn't just rush out.

"Is anybody else up?" I asked.

"Just you and me," he said. "You want eggs? Maybe little cereal?"

"Just coffee, Pa. I want to get to the library early this morning and study a few hours."

I looked warily up the stairs and listened for a moment and followed him into the kitchen. He poured me steaming coffee from the pot and went to the stove for the toast.

"Cold last night," he said. "I get up once to turn up heat."

I took too big a swallow of the coffee and scalded myself and clapped my hand to my mouth to keep from yelling. He had his back turned and didn't notice my agony.

"Pa," I said, and the word came smoking off my tongue. "Mrs. Bratsos has brought Marika here for a marriage contract. Isn't that right?"

He came back to the table and sat down. He buttered his toast slowly for a long moment without speaking and his silence was an answer.

"Jesus, Pa," and my mouth still stung. "That's awful."

He spoke just above a whisper.

"You are young," he said. "Hard to understand that girl wants own home and children. Not many unmarried Greek men in Albuquerque. Aunt Stella and Uncle George have hard time and cannot give things a young girl wants."

"You sure she wants to get married now?"

Pa measured me sternly with his eyes.

"Of course she wants marry," he said. "All girls want marry."

I shook my head, hearing my voice strange and excited.

"You should let her find some fellow she loves. She's not happy about this business. I don't think she wants to get married now."

Pa stared at me hard.

"Why so excited?" he said. "She not have to marry right now, this year. Meet right man and marry later. Why you stirred up hot like iron in ladle?"

I couldn't meet his eyes.

"I just don't think it's right," I said. "The family is hard up and they bring the girl here to sell her. Get some prosperous son-in-law to help them out."

Pa's lips went tight and his cup banged on the table.

"You tell me I help sell slave?" he said, and there was anger in his voice. "If Marika not want to marry, she not have to marry. Uncle George and Aunt Stella write me to speak to few people in city. I not make dirty crime."

"I didn't mean it like that, Pa."

"Spit out what you damn mean."

He was hurt and it wasn't any use. We were talking about different worlds.

"It doesn't matter, Pa," I said, and I rose from the table. "I'll go to work right from the library."

His eyes were puzzled.

"No come home eat lunch?"

"If I get hungry I may grab a bowl of soup outside."

He watched me and was concerned but didn't say another word.

Chapter 6

I SPENT THE MORNING IN THE LIBRARY ACROSS the river leafing through the magazines. A few wheezing old men sat with me around the long reading table with their noses almost touching the pages of their books. At the desk by the door a plaintive-faced librarian sat with her hands folded and might have been dreaming of the world outside.

After a while, to try and stop thinking about Marika, I walked through the stacks of books remembering the hundreds of times I had browsed in them in years gone by. I sat down in a reading chair across from the children's section and watched a little dark-faced Mexican boy on his knees leafing slowly through a book of pictures. Seeing him kneeling there, so young and intent, with his eyes downcast, turned back the years as quickly as if they were pages of an old newspaper caught in some sharp and sudden wind.

It wasn't long, maybe a year or so after Ma died, that Pa found me one night after supper going through some of the library books Mike had brought home. Mike was much further along in school than I and had visited the library a number of times. Neither Pa nor I could believe there were as many books as he said. That night Pa decided it was time for us to see, and he put on my cap and took his hat and we left Mike to wash the dishes.

We walked down Dart Street, and outside the coffee-house some Greek men on their way in called to Pa to join them. For a moment the thought of the glasses of masticha and the cups of hot sweet coffee must have tempted him. He hesitated and looked down at me but I was burning with eagerness for the place of many books. He waved them off and we walked on.

We crossed the river where the long ore boats glistened in the twilight and walked down Barrows Street and came to the old dark brick building with great gleaming windows. Inside the door Pa took off his hat and pulled off my cap, and for what seemed a long time we stood there and waited.

My pa was a maker of steel, a driver of men in mills where mighty fires blazed into the sky. He was a king among the high cranes and seething furnaces. But in the silent and somber library with the unsmiling women walking softly and the high racks laden with thousands of venerable books, he must have felt himself a stranger in an alien land.

Yet he had courage and finally he marched me into the maze of the stacks. We walked slowly through the aisles between the shelves of books. Here and there he stopped and peered closely trying to read one of the titles. He walked on holding my hand and we were both silent with wonder. He stopped and peered again and we turned and started down another aisle and back the way we had come, until it seemed we were lost in a labyrinth of racks with shelves of books.

But one of the unsmiling women had seen us wandering and taken pity and came to offer help. Pa asked for the place of the children's books and first she took us to her desk and gave us cards and Pa signed proudly for both of us. Then we followed her to a section in a corner with the shelves close to the floor. Pa knelt beside me and took a few books carefully and turned the pages showing me the pictures and with some effort, because he was never much of a reader in English, read to me from the text. Once at a passage in *Mother Goose* he laughed out loud and then looked quickly around as if he had suddenly remembered all the signs commanding silence.

When we left the library that night Pa and I each carried an armful of books. After picking out a few for me, he had boldly asked the librarian to direct him to the shelves of philosophy, explaining that he was a Greek and a descendant of Aristotle. He selected several weighty volumes that he carried with dignity to the desk to have them stamped.

Walking out of the library that first time was for me a moment that would never be matched in all the visits to the place I made in the years that followed. I think it was a wonderful moment for the old man too, walking out of the library with his son, carrying an armful of books.

On the way home we stopped in the coffeehouse, and while Pa sipped his masticha and I nibbled a sweet kouloura, the books were heaped neatly on our table and Pa proclaimed loudly to everyone where we had been.

I don't think Pa ever used his library card after that night. Mike returned the unread philosophy books a couple of weeks later complaining because they were heavy. The card must have expired some twelve years now, but Pa kept it on the mantel in the parlor, dusty with age but standing as a testament to his entrance into the world of books and knowledge.

The Mexican boy stared at me out of his big dark eyes, and I smiled at him and saw myself on my knees the way it had once been.

Later, after I bought a hot dog and a glass of root

beer from a vendor, I went to work. Rothstein was rushing around the store, his short fat body spurting between cases and the counters.

"You are late," he said. "I have been busy."

"You are right," I said. "I've been in conference with the mayor."

He turned to Orchowski, the policeman, who sat on an empty case of beer partly hidden behind one of the iceboxes against which he propped his great feet.

"You see what happens when you hire a college boy," Rothstein said. "They get smart-aleck."

Orchowski nodded.

"But he gives the place a shade of class," he said.

Rothstein sniffed the air.

"What's the matter with this place you think it needs class?"

"It needs class," Orchowski said.

"Your head needs class," Rothstein said. "Get your big flat feet out on the street and do some duty."

"Gentlemen," I said and picked up the worn broom, "if we cannot agree I bring this place class, at least let us agree that through my skilled broom work I bring this place a moderately clean floor."

"I will accept that," Rothstein said.

"Has my pa been around?" I asked. "Or my brother?"

"Everybody in the bush in here the past hour," Rothstein said, "except your family." He turned to Orchowski. "I mean it," he said. "Get your big feet off my icebox. You are in here so much, people will think I run a bookie."

Orchowski's big-boned face loosened into a smile and he winked at me.

"All the iceboxes in this place are like the belts holding up your pants," he said to Rothstein. "Any one of 'em can give under pressure at any moment." He bellowed laughter at his humor.

Rothstein shook his head sadly.

"They have opened all the cages," he said, "and put the morons into uniform. The public is defenseless."

A customer came into the store carrying a shopping bag clinking with empty bottles.

Orchowski got heavily to his feet and started to the door.

"I'll see you tonight after I get off," he said to Rothstein. "Save me a couple of cold quarts."

"Go chisel from someone else," Rothstein said.

"I wanna drink you out of business first," Orchowski said and bellowed laughter again as he walked out the door.

"Give me six cans of Pabst," the customer said.

We got busy then for a while until sometime after five o'clock when a lull set in. I swept the floor and was near the front window when I saw Marika. She was standing uncertainly before the store with a small napkin-wrapped package in her hands.

I went quickly out the door and faced her beneath the tinted twilight sky.

"Marika," I said, and there was a sudden warmth in my cheeks remembering the night before. A short distance away a group of children screamed as they played and cars passed swiftly on the darkening street.

"Your father told me where you worked," she said. "He asked me to bring you some supper."

Her voice sounded neither hurt nor accusing but quiet and impersonal. I pointed at the drab front of the store with the neon sign flaming "Discount Liquors."

"I am broom boy and bottle jockey in this palace," I said.

She did not laugh and stood watching the children play, leaving me struggling, thinking of something more to say.

"Marika, listen. We can leave the supper in the store for me later. I'll walk you part of the way home."

Without waiting for an answer I took the wrapped plate and left it in the store. I got my jacket, telling Rothstein I would be back in a few moments.

We walked down the street past the coffeehouses and taverns and saw the lean wild-faced old men over their glasses of masticha preparing for the long night of cards and dancing. We had not spoken to one another since leaving the store.

"Marika, I don't know how to explain," I said. "Last night was a terrible thing for me to do."

She didn't answer and we crossed the street and started through a vacant lot. A gust of cold wind whipped about our faces and I shivered and drew up the collar of my jacket. I kept sneaking glances at her, marveling at the loveliness of her face in profile.

"You know why my mother brought me here," she said, and her voice was a harsh whisper on the twilight. "You know, don't you?"

For a moment I wondered whether to tell her the truth. Then I was afraid she would catch me if I lied.

"I think so."

"You must think that I'm for sale," she said. "Like a cow or a sheep."

"I don't think that," I said quickly. "It's none of my business."

She paused then at the edge of the vacant lot, her cheeks suddenly pale even in the cold.

"You're lying," she said, "and last night was a sampling of the merchandise on sale."

Her words stung as if she had slapped me.

"You're crazy," I said. "Honest to god, it wasn't like that at all."

She watched me silently for a long moment. Beyond the dark roofs of the buildings the night sky glittered and the wind swept scraps of paper along the gutters.

"I'm sorry," I said. "Marika, I'm sorry, but it wasn't the way you think."

"You better go back to work," she said, and her voice became low and quiet.

"Marika, listen."

"I've got to go now," she said, and all the defiance was gone, leaving her face small and weary. "We are having visitors at your house for supper. Mr. Gastis and his sister. They will watch me eating chicken and rice, and if I drink too much wine or laugh too loudly and how I sip my coffee."

"Marika," I said, but she shook her head and turned to leave and then stopped, as if there was more she wanted to say.

"After they leave Mama will ask me what I think," she said, "and your father will ask me what I think, and on their way home the sister of Mr. Gastis will ask him what he thinks."

She didn't look at me again.

"I've got to go," she said. "I'll be late."

I watched her crossing the street, her legs so slender, her slim body bent against the wind.

Walking back to the store through the lot, I remembered Mr. Gastis. A tall man in his late forties or early fifties with a doleful face and a thick wiry fuzz of hair standing up from his lean brown forehead. He had a spinster sister with the face of a witch who kept his house, a large ten-room brick on Cordelia Street. He owned the Galipoli Wholesale Grocery with several warehouses downstate. He was prominent in a number

of Greek lodges, and once at the head of some delega-
tion or other he had his picture in the paper shaking
hands with the mayor.

Mr. Gastis and Marika. It made me feel sick.

I was through in the store at ten. Rothstein closed up
and we cleared the last empty bottles and I swept the
floor for the last time. Orchowski knocked on the locked
door and I let him in. A few moments before eleven I
left them arguing about the Michigan backfield and
walked home.

The front of the house was dark and I walked around
to the back. A light showed through the kitchen window
and I let myself in.

Marika was sitting alone at the table with her slim
fingers pale upon the flowered cloth. Almost at once I
smelled the lingering odor of butted cigars. There was
no sound of movement in the stillness of the house.

"Where is everybody?" I asked and then noticed the
unreal pallor of her cheeks. "What's the matter?"

She leaned slightly forward and stared at her hands.
Weariness shadowed her eyelids and loosened her lips.

"I'm going to be married," she said, "to the wholesale
grocer." She smiled foolishly, her face mocking the
words. "Mama was so pleased. They all left together
with your father taking them home. Mama thought she
would have to talk to me for weeks and weeks and have
me meet several more gentlemen, but I told her in the

131

kitchen while they waited inside that Mr. Gastis would be fine, just fine." She laughed a small, absurd laugh without warmth.

I was shocked and didn't know what to say and something hurt inside me.

"Mama wants us to leave first thing in the morning and carry the good news to Papa. Mr. Gastis and I will write each other for a while to become better acquainted. More genteel that way. Your father was so pleased too."

I felt a quick shame for Pa.

"Jesus, Marika," I said. "You don't have to." I tried furiously to find the right words. "The Greeks may be all crazy but you don't have to do this thing."

"Nobody is making me," she said and paused and her fingers curled into tight little fists on the table. "But Papa is sick and cannot work any longer and I love him so much. Mama tosses in the night and does not sleep and in her own way loves him too and wants what is best for him and it would be all right if I were only not so ashamed." She stopped and looked helplessly at me. "You helped make me feel ashamed," she said.

"I didn't mean it like that," I said desperately. "I don't know why I had to kiss you except maybe because you're so pretty. But you can't do this crazy thing. You can't marry a man so much older."

She stared at me suddenly aroused, her eyes glittering in the slim circles of her face.

"It must be wonderful to have an education," she said. "A college education makes one so smart."

I felt my cheeks burn. "Sure," I said angrily. "At least you learn to figure the difference between twenty and fifty."

Her eyes went beaten in her face and I was sorry the moment the words were out of my mouth. She bobbed her head down in a queer shuddering motion and began to cry.

"I'm sorry," I said. "Marika, please don't cry. I didn't mean that." I knelt beside her chair and tried gently to raise her head. "Listen, Marika," I pleaded. "Please stop crying. It doesn't help to cry."

I began to stroke the softness of her hair. A strange warmth tingled my fingers and I wanted to take her in my arms but I was afraid. Finally the tremblings of her body eased and she straightened in her chair, her eyelids red and a little swollen.

"I'm going to bed," she said and she left the kitchen quickly, almost running up the stairs, and the door of her room closed.

From some yard nearby a dog barked sharply and a house door slammed. I took the decanter of wine from the cupboard shelf and poured a small glass and sipped it slowly.

Her room door opened again and I heard her in the hall and a moment later the bathroom door closed. I counted the seconds and imagined her undressing. There was no sound then until the bathroom door opened and her room door closed again with finality.

I put the decanter of wine away and closed the light and went upstairs. In my room I sat on the edge of my bed in the darkness and could almost feel her awake in the great bed.

In my stocking feet I walked to my window and opened it a few inches. The restive night entered the room. A car passed, the tires humming upon the empty streets, and afterwards the hissing of the mill furnaces came clearly through the night.

I undressed and got into bed. I don't know how long I lay there. The odors of cold night and chilled earth and mill dust gathered slowly in the room. Every so often the clang of a slab striking the rolls jarring the dark with dull thunder. And when the slabs were still for a moment, the sharp restless click of a woman's heels upon the walk and the hoarse laughter of passing men.

I heard my name from within the house. Faint and unreal as if it was the mournful wail of wind under the eaves. I listened unmoving in the darkness.

Until the silence mocked me and I thought it had been a dream, wandering between darkness and sleep. I stirred fitfully, breaking the tight silence, and heard my name again.

I swung out of bed and went to the door and quickly down the dimly lit hall. She stood in the doorway of her room, almost hidden in the shadows, her face a pale blur above the white cloth of her pajamas.

"I fell asleep and had a dream," she said, her voice a shaken whisper. "I woke alone in the dark room, all alone and nothing living or warm around me, nothing caring if I lived or died."

I took her arm feeling her flesh cold.

"You're cold," I said. "Marika, you're so cold."

We walked back into the dark room to the bed.

"Get under the covers," I said, and wanted to stop her trembling.

She moved slowly under the sheet. I pulled the blanket over her knees to her waist and hesitated a little, afraid to sit down.

"Give me your hand, Tony," she said. "Give me your hand." She pulled in her legs and gave me room. I sat down and she turned slightly toward me, her pale cheeks gleaming like dusky flowers.

"Do you want a lamp on?" I asked.

"Not now," she said. "Not as long as you're here."

I held her hand and felt her fingers, the smooth tautness of her wrists and the brittle edges of her nails. We sat like that for moments, wordlessly, until she moved closer, and I placed my hand upon her cheek, upon the high-boned coldness of her face.

"You're so warm," she said. "Your hands are so warm." Her voice rising and falling in the darkness like the uneven whisper of a child. "We will leave in the morning," she said, "to bring Papa the news. And after I am gone will you remember me?"

"You don't have to marry him!" My tongue twisted the words. "Marika, you don't have to marry him!"

"I have to," she said. "With nobody making me I know I have to. Papa and Mama have only me. There's no one else who cares whether they live or die."

I sat silent under the fretful insistence of her voice.

"Would you marry me, Tony?" she said, and the words singed me as if they were fire in the darkness.

"I would," I said. "I would." At that moment it was true because nothing was real beyond the room, the bed of my mother, and the whispering girl.

There was nothing else I could think of to say. A long moment passed before she spoke again.

"He isn't ugly," she said, "and not really old. He spoke of his business that would grow bigger and how he began with one truck that he drove up and down the alleys and called to housewives to buy his fruits. He would buy Mama and Papa a house and I could visit with them whenever I wished. He told me about his big house and how he sometimes sits alone at night and listens to the silence of the empty rooms around him. I could feel his loneliness and couldn't help myself and hated him a little for that."

"Let it alone," I pleaded. "Marika, let it alone."

She moved her head slightly on the pillow and her lips softly brushed my hand. I leaned toward her face, drawn by her cheeks until I felt them moist and no longer cold.

"You are so warm," she said softly.

I kissed the whisper upon her lips and her mouth curled and twisted beneath my own. Close to her I breathed the strange and secret scents of her flesh, the honeyed mouth, the talcumed throat, and all the golden hollows of longing.

"I love you," I said, and the words tumbled fevered from my mouth. "Marika, I love you."

"It's all right," she said, and her fingers touched my cheeks and touched my mouth and touched my eyes. "And you don't have to say you love me."

I kissed her again and the feel of her body out of the folds of blanket searing mine like a torch in the darkness. My own body had a quick and hostile life of its own in a way I had never known, commanding my hands, moving my fingers under the cloth that covered her, upon the soft and springy nipples of her breasts. In that seeking and quivered moment all my barren years bore fruit, and my aching body swept in waves against the coves of her flesh. And at the instant of my furious fumbling to bring us together, the lights of the car turning in before our garage flashed across the walls of the room.

Then I was standing in fear and panic beside the bed. I heard her whimper and the rustle of the sheets and then she stopped. We listened and did not move, and the house about us still and neither of us breathing and then Pa's voice in the kitchen downstairs.

There was only a moment left in the dark room with the mussed bed and the floor cold and hard beneath my bare feet. She sat in the big bed dividing the lines of darkness, her pale face crowned by darkness. I went to her then and knelt beside her on the bed and for one frenzied and voiceless moment we held each other tightly as if we might never let go.

Then I ran from her room and in my own climbed into bed and the sheets were cold as the linen of a shroud and the night was still savage with the remembered feel of her body. As if I had found flesh that belonged to me and had it torn from me again.

I lay for a long while shivering in the dark.

Marika and her mother left for home the next day. I didn't get to see her again. I ran from her once in shame and I ran again in confusion because in the morning nothing made sense and I needed time to think.

I got up at dawn and dressed and left the house. I went quietly out the back door cutting around the bare and tangled shrubs beyond the fence. I looked up for a moment at the window of her room and seemed to see the curtains drawn slightly to one side.

I stood there in the cold early morning with the drab houses rooted to the winter earth, and a gray dead sky touching the rooftops, and a few brown shriveled leaves still scattered across the ground.

I waved and felt something twisting in my body and could not really know if it was Marika and if she waved back. Perhaps the curtains had not moved at all. I turned and walked away.

Chapter 7

I CAME HOME FROM WORK THAT NIGHT AROUND eleven o'clock and found Pa in his robe stirring a big pot of soup simmering on the stove. I could tell it was avgolemono by the tang of lemon that clung to the air.

He looked at me grimly as if there were plenty of questions waiting to be asked but he wanted me fed first.

"I make your favorite," he said. "Avgolemono soup better than Mrs. Lanaras."

I hung my jacket on the hook behind the door and washed my hands in the sink.

"I don't feel much like soup, Pa."

He grunted. "I no ask what in hell you feel like. Sit down and eat hot soup."

I sat down and he ladled from the pot into bowls and brought them steaming to the table. He sat across from me and the vapor rose in clouds between us.

"I eat one bowl before you come," he said. "Now one more bowl, then bowl again when Mike comes from shift. Plenty good soup. Lemon just right. Mrs. Lanaras make avgolemono, never put in enough damn lemon."

"It smells good, Pa."

I couldn't get near my bowl yet, but Pa had already scooped up a big spoonful and tossed it smoking into his mouth as calmly as a circus fire-eater digesting flame. I always marveled how he could stand food so hot. Mike would say when a man had worked in the mills as long as Pa, the heat baked through his flesh and bone.

I waited for my soup to cool and Pa watched me steadily. He finished his soup and I had not yet touched mine. He pushed away his empty bowl and leaned forward and rested his elbows on the table.

"Now boy," he said. "What in hell is matter with you? Yesterday gone all day. Today leave early in morning and not even come back say good-by to friends who leave."

I wanted to tell him about Marika. Every time the words began to form I lost my nerve. I had seen the girl for the first time since we were children, maybe three or four hours in the last two days. How could I make a case for love and hope to sell the old man?

"Pa, don't laugh at me now."

He made a gesture of impatience.

"I will not laugh."

I watched him and he waited.

"I think I love Marika."

He sat stiffly for a moment and then turned his head and coughed with his cheeks trembling.

"You said you wouldn't laugh!" I said angrily.

He quickly managed an expression of innocence.

"I not laugh," he said. His voice softened. "You get tall like weed now but I remember like yesterday when you just little shit. You hang on my hand to coffee-house and I lift you up to chair and old Karkadis, he is waiter who is dead now, bring you koulouraki and you eat and make big pile of crumbs." He paused and could not fully erase a trace of smile that tickled the corner of his mouth. "Now from cookie we come fast to love."

"I know how it sounds," I said. "You think maybe I'm crazy. I fall for her the only time I've seen her since we were children. We only had a few hours to talk. I left the house this morning because I wanted time to think, because I didn't want to say anything I would be sorry for later." I paused almost out of breath. "Pa," and I wanted so much for him to understand. "I know how crazy it sounds, but I think I love her. I think I love Marika."

He stared at me for a long and silent moment and the smile gone from his face.

"Not so crazy," he said and he spoke softly. "While you talk I remember how I see Mama for first time in old country at mountain picnic. She dance in line of women and she small and fair and like flower. I see her then and I say to myself, Angelo, this girl must become wife. I eat

142

souvlakia and bread with both hands and drink plenty wine and not go near because must not talk to girl without family say okay. Talk to girl without family say okay, maybe father, maybe brothers cut your throat, but I think I love her then."

Pa and I were that close I could feel it inside me as cutting as the edge of a sharp knife, the way it must have been long ago on the mountain when he first saw Ma dance.

He snapped back to the present.

"But this little different," he said and frowned. "You got school. You still young man."

"How old were you when you married, Pa?" I asked.

He waved his hand.

"Old enough," he said. "Big, dumb and plenty wild."

"What's holding me back?"

He twisted in his chair.

"This not be so easy," he said. "This be tough nut even for Angelo." He clenched his big hand into a fist and hammered gently on the table. "Aunt Stella want son-in-law with money. Established citizen like Mr. Gastis. I tell her you want only daughter, maybe old lady have stroke."

I had to smile imagining the old hawk's face when she heard about Marika and me. Then suddenly I remembered that I had not really spoken to Marika. I was not sure what her reaction would be, whether she would even want me if she could have me.

"Pa," I said. "I don't really know how Marika feels. I don't want to get married next week anyway. All I want is time to write her and have her write me and see how we both feel. Mr. Gastis will have to wait."

Pa shrugged.

"Gastis wait fifty years," he said. "Few more damn months not kill him." He paused and shook his head. "Maybe better we speak up while girl and mother here. If you tell me in morning maybe we all sit down and talk together."

"I wasn't sure, Pa. I wanted to be sure I wasn't just sorry. I felt sorry for her last night in her room."

He gave me a sudden hard and baleful look.

"When you see girl in room last night?"

I had slipped and quickly tried to cover. Not that I wanted to lie to Pa, but how could I make him, or anyone for that matter, understand about Marika and me in the dark room the night before.

"She had a bad dream, Pa, and she started to cry. I heard her and went to her room and sat with her for a short time."

Pa scratched his chin thoughtfully.

"Nothing happen?" The question hung in the air like a noose.

I felt my back against the wall.

"Just a little bit, Pa," I said and realized how that must sound.

He swallowed against his Adam's apple that bobbed suddenly in his throat.

"What hell you mean by little bit?"

"I just kissed her and that was all. I talked to her awhile and then I kissed her."

He watched me silently for a moment and shook his head.

"By god, boy, you grow up pretty fast. Girl in house few hours and you sit on side of bed and give her big kiss."

I could feel my cheeks flushed.

"It wasn't especially a big kiss. Just a kiss."

He grunted.

"Should be big kiss. When Varinakis give girl kiss should remember family tradition. In old days when Angelo kiss girl, sometime break her neck."

I laughed and Pa smiled.

"Okay," he nodded. "If sure you not dizzy after kiss and sure you not feel sorry for girl who come to marry man like Gastis, I take first step. I write powerful letter in morning. I tell Uncle George and Aunt Stella stop. My college boy son will die if not promised hand of daughter. Just remember one thing."

"What's that, Pa?"

"No talk of marriage until after you get goddam goatskin. If not finish school I break head."

"Okay, Pa, but its sheepskin, not goatskin."

"Don't be damn smart-aleck," he said brusquely.

I looked at Pa and didn't know what else to say. He understood and made a face and laughed.

"You think maybe Papa nuts? You think old man give me plenty trouble when I tell him I meet girl yesterday and love today. Old man knows nothing on love. He thinks all women same in dark. Well, punk, I fool you."

"Pa," and I really was amazed. "I always suspected. You are wiser than Plato and Aristotle together."

He made a generous gesture of protest.

"Not both, boy. Maybe Angelo little wiser than one, but not both."

We laughed together and suddenly I remembered the avgolemono and felt hungry. The soup was cold but I didn't care. Pa watched me and his smile was warm.

"Marika good girl," he said. "I see she not happy. She say yes to mother on Gastis but she not want him." He paused in speculation. "We got little money saved in bank. Not much. Nothing like Gastis, but if girl say yes we help Uncle George all we can. You smart boy. Someday maybe you make more money than old Gastis."

I finished the bowl of soup. Pa was a champion and his faith made me feel a man.

"Now go for bed," he said. "Big love need plenty sleep. Maybe tomorrow you change mind." He went to the stove and raised the flame under the pot. "I wait for Mike," he said. He looked at the clock on the wall and it was a few minutes before midnight.

I left him smiling beside the stove in the worn and faded bathrobe that was at least twenty years old and he would not give up. Mike and I had given him a new one for his last birthday, a resplendent garment in red and black that he never wore.

I walked upstairs to Ma's room and snapped on the light. Everything was as it had always been and yet in some strange way changed.

Pa said Ma had been like a flower, small and fair and perhaps as beautiful as Marika. What I was, and what I felt, they had made in this room of their flesh and by their love. I stood beneath the shadow of the long bed. All this had meaning and order and warmth. Then to the night before in the dark with Marika beside me. From now on this room would belong to us as well as Pa and Ma.

Later, something snapped me out of sleep. I sat up startled in the dark and heard the hot and angry voices from downstairs. I hurried from my room and ran down the shadowed stairs into the kitchen.

Pa and Mike were standing a few feet apart and Pa's face was dark and twisted in terrible anger. Mike stood against him, hard as iron and his fists clenched by his sides.

I could never remember seeing Pa as he looked then and cold fear rubbed my flesh. He was angry, but more than that, as if he had received some blazing blow, cutting deeper into his body than anything he had ever known.

"Pa," I said helplessly. "Jesus Christ, Mike."

Mike spoke to me without taking his eyes off Pa.

"Sheila and me got married tonight."

I heard him and for a moment it didn't make sense and then it did. I shut my eyes tightly and wished myself far away so I would not have to look at Pa again.

"In this goddam way," Pa said and his voice swept with fury, "you walk into house and tell family you marry. After twenty-five years you come in dark night like thief and spit good news."

"I tried to tell you," Mike said, and his own voice shook under an effort to speak quietly. "I told you I wanted to get married but you wouldn't listen. I tried to make you understand I'm not a kid no more. I got a right to make my own life."

Pa looked him up and down as if he were dirt.

"Go make life," he said. "Forget church and house you born in. Forget memory of mother. Forget father and brother and everything but woman you want in bed. To hell with everything else."

"Pa," I said. "Pa, don't make it sound like that." But my voice was a slim tree in a storm.

"Not like that," Mike said savagely. "I don't forget nothing. But I remember more than just the things you want me to remember. All you can remember is how you are a Greek and gonna live like a Greek and make us all die like goddam Greeks!"

"Black day you born!" Pa said, and his face was dark with blood. "Black day in my house when you come from mother! Black goddam day!"

"Curse me," Mike said, and his eyes suddenly hot with fire of their own. "Curse me but remember you mark your own flesh. You curse yourself and the woman that gave me birth. Remember that."

Pa raised his arm and the big hand hooked and became a fist and for one frenzied moment I thought he was going to smash Mike. Then the fist opened and the fingers pointed and condemned as the hand of the God painted by the mad priest in the church.

"Go with your whore!" Pa said, and he spoke through his teeth so the words hissed and smoked. "Go until death from my house!"

Mike shuddered as if Pa had locked teeth in his flesh and loosed a horse cry from his throat. Then in a violent gathering of his body he spit at Pa's feet and stumbled toward the door and rocked it closed behind him.

The kitchen was still except for the labor of Pa's breathing. I touched his arm but wordlessly he shook off my hand. I stepped back and didn't touch him again.

He looked at me but I swear he could not see me. He stood alone and terrible in his grief and pain and I burned for him because there was no way I could help.

He walked from the kitchen. His steps were slow and labored on the stairs.

I stood alone for a long time. Finally I walked up the stairs into the darkened hall. There was light shining under the door of Ma's room. He had carried his grief to her.

I waited in the hall, listening for sound from the room but there was none. In the long moments of silence I tried to believe that what had happened was part of a disordered dream from which I must wake.

The doorbell rang shrilly. My first thought was that Mike had returned and I wanted to call to Pa. He must have heard the bell but there was no movement in the room. I hurried downstairs.

It was Father Kontoyannis looking as if he had been roused from sleep.

"Mike and his wife came by," he said quietly. "They told me about Angelo."

I was grateful that he had come. He took off his coat and wore an old woolen sweater that buttoned in front and showed the gray flannel of underwear at his throat.

"He is upstairs in my mother's room," I said.

I followed him upstairs and waited in the shadows of the landing. He knocked once on the door and called Pa's name. When there was no answer he knocked louder and shook the knob. Finally Pa said something I could not hear clearly and Father Kontoyannis entered the room and closed the door.

I shivered then in the dark cold hall and I was still barefooted in pajamas and went to my room for slippers and robe. Coming back I walked quietly past the room and the priest's voice came in a muffled and uneven whisper through the door.

In the kitchen I put water and coffee in the pot and set it over a burner on the stove. While I waited I wondered where Mike and Sheila had gone. Their wedding night in pain and sorrow. Yet they had stopped for the priest because Mike loved Pa as I did. He might spit in anger but he could not erase the memory of the warm years in Pa's shadow. Or could he? A chill carried down my back. Perhaps this was the way a family was broken.

The coffee began to perk in the pot. The boiling bubbles rose and burst in the glass top, slowly at first and then more quickly.

Someone came down the stairs and in a moment Father Kontoyannis walked into the kitchen. Out of the dark hall into the light his face was unguarded and reflected anguish in sharing the burdens of other men. Then the mask returned and he smiled.

"The coffee smells good," he said.

He sat down and clasped his hands. I took cups from the shelf and poured coffee and sat down across from him.

"He is angry and bitter," the priest said. "He feels Mike has betrayed him. It will take a while before this is eased. How long," he shook his head slowly, "how long depends on Angelo and Mike and the girl."

"Father, what can I do to help?"

He sipped the hot coffee, his deep dark eyes framed between pale cheeks and white hair.

"There is little that can be done," he said, "against the old country village distrust of the stranger, against the stubborn parent trying to hold sons and daughters loyal to the past." His voice sounded low and far away. "But the young are impatient and feel no allegiance to what has been true for their fathers. They pull angrily from the past and the bitterness takes months and years and sometimes never heals. I remember a boy, the son of a Greek grocer in our parish, who married a girl with the blood of Saul and David in her veins. The father burned photographs and clothing of his son and in the ten years before he died never mentioned the boy again."

I sat burdened under the vision of the unforgiving grocer. Pa and Mike and their bitterness to be healed.

"God could not talk to Job," the priest said slowly, "not because he was unjust and without pity for his suffering but because a father cannot really talk to his son. Abraham could not make Isaac understand the covenant of sacrifice. All man's life is a search for the father he has lost from birth."

He stood up and looked wearied again.

"Thank you for the coffee," he said, and he gently

touched my arm. "Poor Tony," he said. "Sometimes the youngest has it hardest of all."

I helped him with his coat. He looked once back upstairs.

"Try and be patient with him," he said. "Even in anger men like Angelo are a breed apart. When they are gone a race of giants will have passed from the earth."

"Good night, Father," I said, and only after the door was closed did I mind I had not spoken words to thank him.

I turned out the lights and went upstairs. Light still shone under the door of Ma's room. I wanted to go to him and then remembered how he shook off my hand.

I went to my room and to my bed. I thought of Mike and Sheila and Marika far away. Of the family we had been, our lives twined like the strands of a rope, and wondered if we would ever have that closeness again. Mostly I thought of the old man sitting alone in Ma's room grieving the passing of the old ways.

I cried a little then, holding my face deep in my pillow so he would not hear.

Chapter 8

PA AND I TRIED TO MAKE CHRISTMAS FESTIVE FOR each other. I bought a small tree from Karpetsou and decorated it with lights and tinsel and artificial snow. Pa put a glittering wreath of green holly on the front door and hung another one in the kitchen window.

On Christmas morning I gave him a wallet and a pair of slippers and he gave me a fine fleece-lined jacket that he had bought weeks before. There was another jacket for Mike unopened in a box at the top of the closet in his room. We went through the motions of actors in a play but neither Pa nor I felt much like Christmas.

The morning after that night when he drove Mike from the house, I found Pa in the kitchen with coffee on the stove. His eyes were circled with dark and weary shadows and he looked old and without the zest that always marked him for me.

Once during that morning, unable to keep silent, I

tried to speak of what had happened, thinking it might be better if he talked his resentment out.

"We will not speak of that," he said and he spoke quietly. "Mike gone now from this house."

I let him alone. As much afraid of hurting him more as I was of rousing his anger.

True to his word, that afternoon he sat down and wrote a long letter to Aunt Stella and Uncle George. He would not show me what he had written but I could not imagine the eight pages he filled with his scrawl were all pleas for my love of Marika. I think some of his rampant bitterness must have siphoned off into the letter to old country people who could sympathize and understand. The ingratitude of children. The raising of vipers in the bosom of the family.

I wrote to Marika that day as well, hoping her mother let her mail alone. I wrote that I had spoken to Pa and that he understood because he had seen Ma for the first time and known almost at once that he loved her. In writing I stopped many times remembering her sad-eyed face against the pillow of the great bed. Then I wrote much more that on paper seemed so different from anything I would have had the courage to say. Finally I asked her to wait, to give us both a chance, to write me soon how she felt.

Rothsteins was open until six in the evening on Christmas Day and I worked until closing. Almost a week had passed since the night Mike and Sheila had married and I had heard nothing from them. I had checked with a couple of the boys on his turn and had them relay a message that I wanted to see him. Several days had passed without a word. So all the bright store windows and lights of holiday trees and boisterous santas ringing dull bells on the corners beside their pots seemed to mock my misery.

Sometime before closing on Christmas Day I saw Mike's car in the street outside the store. I got my jacket quickly and told Rothstein I wanted to leave. He waved me out and gave me a pint of cherry brandy as a present.

When I opened the door of the car, Sheila and Mike were together. I got in and closed the door.

For a long moment no one spoke and then Sheila reached over and kissed me on the cheek.

"Merry Christmas, brother," she said.

"Merry Christmas," I said.

"Merry Christmas," Mike said gruffly.

I smiled at him and his face seemed thinner than I remembered.

"How is your father?" Sheila asked.

"He's better now," I tried to find the right words. "Honest to god, he's better now."

Mike shook his head and stared at his hands locked around the wheel.

"The damn things he said to me," Mike said.

"The old man is hot tempered," I said. "You know how he is."

"I saw him a few days ago at the alloy mill," Mike said. "I was coming from the conditioning dock with Barut and he came from the shears. He saw me and never said a word. He turned his back on me and cut me dead like I was some kind of dog." He finished and laughed mockingly.

"Mike," Sheila said.

He looked at her and then winked at me.

"I guess you want to know why we took the big step," he said. "I got tired of waiting. Tired of wondering how I was going to work it out with the old man. Tired of making excuses. I just got good goddam tired."

"That isn't all," Sheila said. "Mike, tell him the truth."

Mike watched her steadily for a moment and did not speak.

"We are going to have a baby," Sheila said.

"You feel better?" Mike asked and he sounded a little angry. "Jesus Christ, if the old man only knew that." He shook his head in cold and silent laughter.

My astonishment must have showed on my face because Sheila smiled gently and patted my hand.

"He is your brother," she said to Mike. "I want him to know the truth."

That helped me understand why Mike should have

decided so quickly. Then I thought painfully of Pa and what he would say if he knew.

"Can you imagine anything so damn crazy?" Mike said. "She talks like I married her to make an honest woman out of her. I been pushing her for months and she's been stalling. I finally talked her into getting the license and that night we were going to come home first and talk to the old man. But I knew what he would be like. Nobody in the world worthy of Big Angelo and his boys. He would have started swinging two thousand years of damn Greek history in our faces. I took her to a justice and we got married."

"I waited outside in the car that night," she said. "He wanted to tell your father alone."

"I think the worst thing was spitting at him," Mike said. "Jesus Christ!" He put his knuckles to his mouth and rubbed hard against his lips.

"Pa has got a temper," I said. "He must be sorry for things he said that night."

"Did he say he was sorry?" Mike asked.

I had to shake my head. Mike laughed.

"Not the old man. Not Angelo Varinakis. He can kick you half to death but a Greek like Angelo doesn't feel sorry."

I twisted in my seat feeling in a way I should defend Pa before Sheila.

"He believes in things a certain way," I said. "It's hard to get him to change."

"We sent the priest that night," Sheila said.

"It was her idea," Mike said.

"He spoke a little to us," she said. "He is an understanding man."

Inside the liquor store Rothstein had come to the front to lock up. The door had a faulty catch and for a moment he pushed hard with his short fat body flattened against the frame, a great balloon across the glass. Then he snapped off the flaming neon sign and the street darkened and the twilight shadows wrapped about the car.

"We can't just keep sitting here," Mike said.

"Let's show Tony our apartment," Sheila said and turned to me. "So far we only have a bed and some kitchen pieces but we have furniture ordered."

"It's not much of a place," Mike said. "Christmas is a hell of a time to find a flat." He turned the key and the motor rumbled. "You got beer," he said to Sheila, "or shall I get some inside?"

"We got beer," Sheila said forcefully and I laughed.

We drove silently for several blocks through the evening streets until Mike parked before an old frame building on a shabby street near the Burly gate. In the house we walked up a flight of stairs that creaked noisily beneath our feet. At the top Mike fumbled with a key and opened the door.

We entered a large bare room empty except for an

armchair in one corner and a small multi-lighted Christmas tree beside the window.

"Merry Christmas," Sheila said brightly.

"Merry Christmas," I said and felt sharply sorry for them. There were the warm rooms of our house and the great bed in Ma's room against this bare room in a bleak strange house.

"Come in here," Sheila said. I followed her into a small kitchen. In one corner a big ancient black-burnered stove loomed next to a slightly lopsided sink on three legs and a prop of wood. A pitted icebox with enamel chipped from the sides stood beside a worn wooden table with two chairs. But there were clean starched curtains over the single small window and one wall of the kitchen was freshly painted and decorated with a copper wall planter holding a cluster of bright flowers.

"Mike changes turns the beginning of the week and has two days off," Sheila said. "We'll finish painting the kitchen then. And we are getting a beautiful new stove. You should see it. It has different colored lights and all kinds of gadgets."

Her cheeks were flushed with excitement.

"But you only have two kitchen chairs," I said. "What about another chair?"

"Only two of us live here," Sheila said and she smiled showing white and even teeth.

Mike had followed us in and he patted her gently on the stomach.

"Won't be two for long," he said and laughed. He started to the icebox. "I'll open a couple of beers. Maybe bread and cheese too."

Sheila motioned me to a chair. "Don't worry about us," she said. "I'll sit on Mike."

I sat down and Mike brought the beer and bread and cheese to the table. He sat down in the other chair and Sheila settled herself on his lap. I drank from the can and felt the cold beer refreshing in my mouth.

"Our first guest," Mike said, "and the slob doesn't even offer a toast."

I choked in the middle of a swallow and Sheila laughed.

"Forgive me," I said. "Do you want the toast in Russian or Turkish or Arabic?"

"Give us that Rothstein special," Mike said. "Now is the time."

"I'll think of a better one," I said.

"What is the Rothstein special?" Sheila asked.

"Go ahead," Mike said. "Just toast me."

"It's Rothstein's lament for Orchowski, the cop that hangs around the store," I said. I raised the can of beer. "To your wooden head. May God protect you from woodpeckers and termites."

They both laughed and the mingling of their voices in mirth was pleasant and reassuring. In a way I would have liked to tell them about Marika, but I was ashamed. I didn't want to beat them with Pa's quick approval of a girl because she was Greek and of a family he knew.

"When we have our kitchen fully painted," Sheila said, "and have our new stove you will come to dinner. We might even invest in a third chair."

"Hooray," I said.

"Sure," Mike said and he stared slowly around. "Next time wear a tux and dress shirt."

Sheila looked at him with concern in her cheeks. I knew my brother and tasted his cup of bitterness.

"It will be different painted and with our new stove," she said.

Mike clenched his fist and hit the table lightly. The gesture reminded me of Pa.

"The old man won't be different," he said. "He doesn't change and he doesn't forget. We spent our wedding night in a lousy hotel and then we take this flat because we got to have a place to live fast. But all the time the old man goes his own way. Sleep in the goddam street for all he cares."

Sheila got off Mike's lap. She stood in the center of the kitchen facing him.

"Mike Varinakis, you can go to hell," she said. "If your spirit is the best I can get from a descendant of

Pericles, I should have married a red-haired man from County Clare."

Mike's face twisted in a crooked grin.

"Look at her," he said. "Sassy and pregnant and telling me off."

"That's right," Sheila said and winked at me and made a face. "I'm weary of your histories. Where do you Greeks get off? You think you have the only heroes? You think your fathers are the only ones with an old country to be nostalgic about? Let me tell you, my buckos, we not only have heroes like the Rolands and the Beowulfs, but we have Dublin and Limerick and the beautiful Shannon and leprechauns and epics like the 'Cattle Raid of Cooley.' "

"Yaaa," Mike snickered. "You got donkeys too and four people ride one at the same time."

"What's the 'Cattle Raid of Cooley'?" I asked.

"That's a story about two oversized bulls who ripped hell out of Ireland," Mike said.

"This will stagger Simonakis," I said. "He has always sworn the bulls belonged to Crete."

They both laughed and Mike took her in his arms. He kissed her soundly and then held her off and admired her.

"You should have talked to the old man that night," he said. "I should have waited in the car."

"Right," Sheila said. "I would have told him all he knows of Ireland was St. Patrick's Day and O'Brien, the

poor old policeman on the corner. I would have told
him what my father used to say about the sweet smell of
burning peat when the colored leaves fall on Dublin."

"Jesus Christ, stop!" Mike said. "Now you sound like
him and Simonakis together." They stood laughing and
it was warm to see them loving in their half-painted
kitchen with fresh starched curtains on the window.
Mike kissed her again and held her tight as if he had
forgotten I was there.

"I better go," I said.

"Have another beer," Mike said. "Drink to the union
of Ireland and Greece. Drink to the 'Cattle Raid of
Cooley.'"

"Pa will be waiting for me," I said.

"Tell him hello for me," Mike said and a trace of
bitterness returned to his voice. "Wish him Merry
Christmas from his eldest son."

I looked helplessly at him for a moment and there was
nothing I could say. Sheila walked with me to the door.
We stood on the landing in the hall and she closed the
door and spoke in a whisper.

"What kind of a man is it?" she said, and the bravado
was gone and the grief evident across her cheeks. "What
kind of a man who can stick knives into his son's flesh."
She stopped and mutely shook her head. Then she kissed
me and held my arms tightly for a moment. "Only you
can help us now," she said.

*   *   *

When I got home I found Pa and Simonakis playing checkers in the kitchen. They were bent grimly and silently over the board. Pa greeted me but Simonakis merely grunted, not bothering to raise his bald bony head.

I got some ham from the icebox to make a sandwich.

"Mrs. Lanaras send soup," Pa said. "In jar beside stove. Put in pot and heat."

"Not now, Pa."

Simnakis made a move and Pa looked back to the board. In a moment he made a counter move.

"Jump," Pa said and there was wicked pleasure on his face.

It rubbed me the wrong way. I had always enjoyed Pa and Simonakis as if they were wild animals at each other's flesh across the board. But I had just come from Mike and Sheila. It seemed wrong that even for a short while our house should seem concerned with nothing more than who would win at checkers.

Simonakis looked up shocked and breathing hard.

"Jump," Pa said. "Dig deep grave."

Simonakis waved his long and thin arm angrily.

"I can see," he said. "I don't need you to tell me what happens on the board. You play your game and let me play mine."

"Sure," Pa said, and he was smiling. "But way you play shows old head not screwed on straight."

Simonakis stared at Pa with his eyes sharp as knives.

"You have a big mouth," he said. "You know, Angelo, you have a big mouth. You think because you win once it makes you a more skilled player. How about all the times I beat you?"

Pa smirked and looked up to include me in his pleasure.

"So long since you win," Pa said. "Hard for me remember what is like to lose."

Simonakis shot out of his chair with his cheeks quivering in outrage.

"I do not have to sit here and be insulted," he said. "I will not finish the game. I am through."

Pa frowned and made a harsh noise through his lips.

"Sit down and make last move."

"I will not sit down!"

Pa waved to me.

"Tony bring glass of wine to poor loser."

I wanted to tell him to hell with the wine and something hard stuck in my throat. I moved then and got the bottle and an empty glass.

Simonakis motioned refusal fiercely.

"Nothing, Tony," he walked sternly away from the table. "I am going home."

Pa shook a warning fist.

"Sit down and make last move," he said, "or maybe you go to hospital for broken nose."

Simonakis snarled from the back door.

"You go to hell, Angelo!" he cried. "I got better things

166

to do than play checkers with a boob kerata like you!"

Pa got red in the face and rose from his chair.

"I no go to hell!" he shouted. "Too many your relatives there!"

Simonakis slammed the door closed behind him.

Pa sat down again muttering under his breath and then glanced at me. I stood unsmiling and suddenly he seemed embarrassed. He swept the checkers off the board and slowly began to put them in the box.

"We just fool around," he said without looking up. "We have little fun."

"Sure," I said. I put the bottle of wine back on the shelf and started to leave the kitchen. Pa called me back.

"You not finish make sandwich?"

For a long moment I did not answer. We stared at each other and he was puzzled and concerned. Then something hurt and angry snapped inside me and I did not care.

"Pa, I saw Mike tonight."

His eyes, watching me, wavered. I pressed him and for the first time felt myself almost a stranger in his house.

"They are living in a shabby apartment," I said. "Today is Christmas and they have nothing but a table and two chairs and some empty rooms."

I was surprised at the hard and flat sound of my voice. Pa's cheeks were suddenly dark and the bones stirred beneath his flesh.

"Your brother make own bed," he said, and his tone cold and unyielding. "Let him now eat own head."

"It's easy to send him to hell," I said and wanted my words as relentless as his own. "But not so long ago we were a family. Maybe you have forgotten."

Pa brought his fist down hard across the table. The box of checkers jumped and a stray one fell off the table and hit the floor and rolled a short distance away.

"I no send him to hell!" he said. "He spit at me! He send me to hell!"

"He was angry," and I felt the furious pounding of my heart. "He's got a temper like you."

Pa watched me and was breathing hard.

"I give that boy love and sweat and my heart," he said. "Now he is big and tough and find woman to say he is man, so he spit!" He paused and violently shook his head. "He spit on his father!"

"Pa," and I was pleading with him then. "You got to try and understand. He loved this girl and wanted to marry her."

"He marry in hell!" Pa said wrathfully. "He spit at me and mother who gave him life. He spit at church and house where he grow. Woman blind his eyes and he see nothing but leg and breast!"

The two of us against each other just as Mike and he had faced each other on that night. That cut my wind and the frenzied need to make him understand was driven from me. Pa was the way he was. I loved him and for a moment felt unbridled anger at Mike and Sheila for bringing me to this pass.

"Never mind, Pa," I said. "Let's leave it alone."

He shook his head slowly. When he spoke his voice was soft and the anger was gone.

"Tony, understand," he said. "I love that boy like I love you. You are both my heart and blood. But you are both of Greek house and faith. Is not right turn claws on family and bring bad blood on house."

"But are we only Greek, Pa?" I said and spoke as quietly as he had. "Mike and I were born in this country. We went to school with Irish and Polish and Jewish boys and girls. They have their traditions and their faiths. How can I be a teacher and still say only Greeks make good wives and good husbands, only Greeks worship God in the right way."

He did not move and for a long moment did not answer. I watched him struggling to find the words to explain and I remembered again the wild old men in the coffeehouse and the way they sang of the past. The old country was real and for them the warming legends never died.

"I no say others not good," Pa said finally. "I work with Irish and Polish and Jewish friends too. But when it comes to marry and live with woman I leave them alone and let them leave me and sons alone."

"That may be all right for you, Pa," I said. "But Mike is gone from our house and you didn't get your way.

You can't force a man to do what you want just because you think it is right. All you can do is drive him away."

We stood silent and I heard the thin hum of the icebox and saw the black checker where it had fallen. I marked Pa's face and wanted to close my eyes, but I had gone too far to turn back. Even Pa knew that.

"All right," Pa said, and he drew a deep breath. "No more talk now."

He started walking from the kitchen and I moved aside to let him pass. Beside me he stopped and his face with the lines of age carved into his cheeks and around his eyes was close to mine. He put his hand hesitantly on my arm.

"For long time young son is little shit," he said. "Then he grow skinny and tall and still is boy, and then one day he is boy no longer, he has become man." He paused and smiled a warm sad smile that burned like sunlight across his face. "On that day father feel like old, old man."

He walked through the hall to his chair in the parlor. In that moment I think I loved him more than I had ever loved him before.

Chapter 9

IN JANUARY THE BLEAK AND COLD DAYS RAN TO-gether as if they were shadows. The crust of the earth was frozen and the life beneath it asleep. In the nights the rumble and hiss of the mills scattered the clear cold air. The streets were deserted early and only the prowling tomcats were left to howl their midnight love beside the back-yard fences. In the morning the windows were laced with frost and I went to school wearing a woolen muffler wrapped around my throat and furred gloves on my hands.

In the beginning of January we received our first letters from Alburquerque. A letter to me from Marika and letters from her mother and father to Pa.

My letter, in a clear slim handwriting, told me she would write and wait. She would be happy if things worked out well for us. She thought of me often.

The day the letter arrived I must have read it fifty times. In the kitchen in the morning over a bowl of steaming farina. On the bus beside the faceless men and women of winter huddled in their coats. In class with the pages hidden between the covers of a notebook. Back home that night, locked in my room, while the wind rocked against the windows.

The letter from her mother to Pa was a missile of thunder and denunciation. Pa would not show it to me, but I watched him as he read it and he shook his head and now and then winced and muttered curses under his breath.

The letter from her father, Pa read to me smiling. Uncle George was happy that his daughter and Pa's son might match. Marika spoke very well of me. They were having a little trouble with her mother — here Pa stopped and gave me a wry grin — but they hoped to work it out. He sent us his love.

In February the weather seemed less cold although the earth was just as raw and desolate. Sometimes in the night the snow fell silently, and at dawn, when the alarm woke me, the ground and rooftops were covered with white untrampled flakes and the drifts swept into graceful ridges and cliffs against the fences.

In February I beat my head in concentration for my term exams. In just a few more months I would receive my degree and had already begun to write my letters soliciting a teaching position in the fall.

With graduation so close, and missing Mike from the house, and all the moments thinking of Marika as well, it was in that winter as if my youth had faltered somewhere behind me and left me to walk on alone. When I arrived home weary from school in the evening I usually found Pa playing checkers with Simonakis in the warm kitchen. They sat for hours, night after night, as if they were two drowsy and torpid bears in hibernation for the winter, stirring awake long enough to make a careful move, slouch to the can, or drink a glass of wine.

That week of my exams Pa roused himself sufficiently to ask anxiously several times how things were going. I reassured him with a confidence I did not always feel, and then had a bowl of soup from the pot simmering on the stove and some of the roast which Mrs. Lanaras had prepared. Afterwards I said a good night which neither of them heard and went to my room, and lay across my bed to read some of Marika's letters again. By then we were writing three and four times a week. She wrote of her years from childhood and some of the secrets she had locked in her heart. I wrote her of my years with Pa and Mike and the anger that split us as a family. So in this way we unfolded our past and revealed our present, and as letters kept going back and forth, we began slowly and cautiously to probe the future, into a time when we would be together. This was something I yearned for more and more with each day and night so that long after my light was out I lay awake and watched the glowing and misty ring around the big pale moon. In that soft and secret glitter I imagined her again in my arms and heard her whisper in the darkness and finally closed my eyes to dream my wild whirling dreams.

I ate supper with Mike and Sheila several evenings a week. I guess Pa knew where I had been when I came home late, but he never asked, and gave me no cause to speak. Almost overnight Sheila had begun to look pregnant with her stomach become a round little melon that was a source of delight to Mike. He could not keep from caressing and patting it, and when I could not help myself and flushed they laughed at me and I had to laugh at myself. I watched them together and vicariously savored their love and anticipated my own.

One evening, when their warm abundance of affection overcame my fear of arousing their resentment, I told them about Marika. That was a festive night. Mike went for wine and we toasted each other endlessly. We drank too much, even Sheila, and Mike had to put her to bed. Afterwards he drove me home but let me out at the corner and remained beyond the boundaries of our street as if it enclosed a strange and unknown land.

It was a springing night, when reckless courage flowed in me, and I might have challenged Pa again but he was at the mill. My edge dulled quickly before the still and empty rooms.

Again there were those nights when Mike seemed

stricken with restlessness and could not sit for long and walked from the lighted kitchen into the darkness of the parlor. Sheila sat silently with her eyes troubled and the food was bitter and tasteless in my mouth.

In a way this disorder was repeated in our house where sometimes late at night after Simonakis had gone, I heard Pa entering Ma's room to sit in there silently for a long while. He never mentioned Mike but I knew how badly he missed him. Mike was an extension of the old man's strength and fire and the violence between them was flesh warring on itself. I missed Mike in our house too, but at least I saw him and Sheila often, and I had my own love fruitful as the earth beneath the frozen crust of winter that waited for the spring.

In March the sky was still sullen. The rain fell on and off in dirty drizzlings across the walks and roofs and ran dirty streams into the corner sewers. Sometimes at night great winds came howling from the bowels of the earth and shook the house and I thought this must be the way in which winter was subdued and the earth loosened and awakened to meet the spring.

And as the earth that stirred and waited, in that month Sheila's body rounded like the arc of the moon. Sometimes in the evening with the three of us at the table in the kitchen I would watch her cautiously and know she was not listening to anything Mike and I were saying. She sat locked within herself, a strange and secret smile lingering for long moments on her cheeks.

As if in some purposeful way men could never understand, she was attending the life which stirred within her.

In April the winds hummed in a lower key and in the dawn the light came early. I heard the massed flights of birds passing above in the night and just before daybreak the shrill-throated song of early sparrows.

At the end of April, Marika and her mother came back to our city. The battle had been as hard and long as the winter, but in the end Pa and I and Marika and her father won out. Pa sent train tickets and they came to seal our engagement and plan for our marriage in the summer.

On a Saturday afternoon in the last week of April, Pa and I, sporting our best suits, met them at the station. We waited in the crowd under the great hollow dome and the redcaps with baggage-laden arms lunged past. When the train was announced we walked down the ramp in time to see it emerge in smoke out of the black tunnel with a single light in front leading the way.

In those last few moments I was fearful that somewhere on the long journey they had changed their minds and started back. There was also an image of a girl built up in the months of letters that might now be broken.

When I saw them everything else was driven from my mind. I waved and hollered and Pa gave me a warning look as if to suggest I compose myself, and then he saw them too. He smiled and waved and finally gave a resounding hoot that startled an old man in a broad-brimmed felt hat who glared at Pa, and we started down the platform to meet them.

There was noise and confusion the length of the train and then we reached them and stopped. Her smile came quickly, shy and bold, and after the cold and lonely months there was a tingling intimacy in being close enough to see her red full lips and pale cheeks and the dark softness of hair much longer than I remembered.

Pa kissed Mrs. Bratsos and kissed Marika soundly. Mrs. Bratsos gave me her cold and clammy cheek and then Marika and I stood looking at each other again without having said a word. She wore a brown cloth coat with a soft-sheened little fur collar about her throat.

Pa gave me a push.

"What is matter with you? Pretty girl come thousand miles see fat head and you stand and look."

"Don't push me," I said, but I kept staring at her and for a moment that was enough. Then because they were waiting we came together and she raised her face and the shy and bold smile for me alone. I kissed her lightly and teased my lips with the nearness of her flesh and savored the warmth of her mouth.

"By god," Pa said. "You kiss like policeman wait to take you away. Shame to Varinakis name."

Mrs. Bratsos stared at him coldly.

"Angelo," she said. "Not so loud and please not to be so coarse."

Pa shrugged that off and we got the suitcases from the porter and walked to the taxi stand. All the way home Mrs. Bratsos rattled on about the shame of having had to inform Mr. Gastis and his sister that all was off. He had written a very stirring letter, she said, complaining he had been badly treated. She spoke of him with an air of grieving. For a moment, only a moment, I felt sorry for the old lady. As if she sensed what I was thinking she gave me a cutting look and said loudly she did not mind because her daughter's happiness came first. Besides, George seemed pleased and was somehow feeling a little better, not well, no, certainly not well, but better. She kept on and on until it seemed her voice created enough pressure to blow apart the taxi and even the driver squirmed behind his wheel.

We carried the suitcases into the house and then I told Pa and Mrs. Bratsos that Marika and I would take a walk. Before the old lady could begin to voice objections Pa took her arm and bustled her into the kitchen to taste some of his avgolemono made especially for their visit.

Marika and I quickly left the house and then we were finally alone. I held her hand and pulled her along. At the corner we turned and walked away from the mills.

"There is a small park a couple of blocks away," I

said. "A small pavilion and a few benches beside some trees."

"Is it a favorite place with you?" she asked. "I have places like that back home. Secret places."

"Only in the winter," I said. "In the summer it's about as secret as Union Station. All the families in the bush pile in."

We crossed Aron Street and passed Bimarski's Bakery which featured cakes for Polish weddings and had a placard in the window announcing a big polka night at the Podmokly Ballroom on the first Tuesday in May.

We entered the park and it was deserted and desolate under the gray winter sky. The water fountain stood forgotten and the benches hinged to the walk were soiled and battered by winter. In the shelter of the pavilion we finally stopped and faced each other.

"You have changed," I said.

"Not really," she shook her head.

"You've let your hair grow," I said, and marveled how rich and black it fell about her cheeks.

"Do you like it?"

"I like it very much."

We were silent for a moment and her eyes searched my own.

"Do you remember that last morning in your house?" She paused an uneasy moment for breath. "I heard you leaving and wanted to come downstairs. I didn't because I was ashamed. I watched you from the window."

"Nothing to be ashamed of," I said boldly. "Marika, that night was beautiful."

"You were so warm," she said softly, and she took my hand and touched my fingers.

I remembered that night and all the lonely nights of winter since then. Into this moment beneath the shadow of the pavilion in the still and deserted park with the first scents of spring stirring about our heads.

"Tony," she spoke faintly in almost a whisper. "Have you ever been with a girl like that?"

There was no mistaking what she meant. I felt a sudden knotting in my stomach. If I told her the truth she might think me inexperienced and immature with no claim to manhood.

"I'm sorry," she said, and her cheeks flamed. "Mama is right when she calls me a hussy."

I took a deep breath.

"Marika, I've never been with a girl all the way." Almost at once the agony of my admission convulsed me. "But I've come awful close with a lot of girls," I said grimly. "I've come close."

She turned slightly away and I peered anxiously at her face above the ringed fur collar and couldn't tell if she was impressed.

"I've never been all the way with a boy either." She spoke seriously and looked at me intently.

"I knew that," I said.

She frowned.

"How did you know?"

The question bumped me back.

"I guess I just knew."

Her lips set firmly in annoyance.

"Well I've come pretty close too. A lot of times."

We stared at each other for a long and soberly balanced moment and then she smiled. I felt a laugh bubbling up my throat and we both laughed long and loud and the echoes rollicked off the gray stone walls around us.

When I could catch my breath I tapped the tip of her nose with my finger.

"You looked so serious," I said.

"You too."

"Not as serious as you."

With a ridiculous expression, a popping of her eyes and a twisting of her lips, she mimicked my voice.

"I've come close with lots of girls," she said archly. "Maybe even a thousand. Maybe two thousand."

"Cut it out," I said and almost doubled up in laughter.

"I don't want you to feel you're getting cheated when you get me," she said, and she shook her head firmly, trembling her black hair. "I know all men prefer women with experience."

"When a fellow gets married," I said, "he wants to be able to choose from women that have been around, all around."

"Salome and Bathsheba?" she asked.

"Marika Bratsos," I said.

A strange and drawn silence settled over us and over the earth around us. For the first time since entering the pavilion I felt the wind faint and restless, and knew she felt it too. Her eyes were large and watchful and we did not speak but listened for the wind and when it swelled again she came abruptly and defiantly into my arms. She raised her face to be kissed and I kissed her and tasted the honey of her mouth and felt the sharp sweet sting of her tongue drawing deep into the marrow of my bones. Then she pulled away and stared at me earnestly.

"Do I kiss well?" she asked.

"Sure," I said and smiled.

"As good as any girl you've ever kissed?"

"Sure."

"Swear it," she said. "On your honor."

"I swear I think you're a little crazy."

"Swear it!"

"I swear," I said.

She laughed in delighted triumph and brushed my cheek with her lips. I put my arms around her and held her tight.

We stood that way under the shadow of the stone pavilion in the park that was a winter island and the city seemed far away. No sound about us but that of the wind and no movement but that of the brittle branches quivering against the sky.

"I'm glad," she said fiercely, and her voice breath-warm upon my throat. "I'm so glad for you and your father. You don't know how Mama carried on, how she hollered at Papa and me in the beginning. The things she accused me of doing and how disappointed she was."

"She sounds as if she is still disappointed."

"I suppose a little," Marika said ruefully. "I think she feels it would have been better for Papa and her with Mr. Gastis, but she knows I am happier and Papa is pleased and she has resigned herself. Poor Mama, she has had so little all her life and wanted so much."

For a long moment we stood silent.

"I will try to make you happy," I said. "A teacher does not make a lot of money and we may never be rich but I will care for you and love you."

"I know," she said softly. "And I will care for you and love you."

Across the edge of the city a dark strip of twilight rimmed the sky. The shadows lengthened about us. The far-off sounds of the mill carried on the sweep of the rising wind. It was an uneasy and darkening moment as it must have been when man was young upon the earth and had only his woman beside him against the coming of the fitful and unknown night.

"I feel strange," I said. "As if we are standing alone in another time and place."

"That's love," she said firmly.

"You are smart," I said. "You have a mind like a whip."

"I have a good mind."

"Sure," I said.

"I'm not just a body."

I grinned at her in the twilight.

"The body part is just more evident," I said.

"If you like girls with big breasts," she said softly, "I don't have big breasts."

"I like you just the way you are."

"I have nice legs and a pleasing face when I'm not frowning," she said, "but I don't have big breasts."

"I like you fine."

"Just so you know," she said. "If you want to back out, now is your chance."

"Back out?"

"Just try," she said.

I pulled her to me and kissed her, a long hard kiss and her body tight against mine and her mouth cold for a second and then warm under my own. And in that moment the lights along the walk glowed on and misted her cheeks and her soft black hair.

That night we sat around the table at supper which Mrs. Bratsos had cooked. Roast lamb hot with the scents of clove and garlic, and lightly browned potatoes in a rich clear gravy.

Simonakis sat licking his lips in expectation as Pa

carved the succulent meat. A place had been set for Father Kontoyannis but the hour at which he had been asked to come had passed. He often had to make unexpected sick calls, so after we waited awhile and the lamb done, Pa suggested we eat and save a good portion for the priest.

"I have not tasted lamb like this for a long time," Simonakis said reverently. "It is food for the gods."

"You should have married," Mrs. Bratsos said. "You could have had lamb such as this and pilaf all the time."

Simonakis sighed.

"It is true," he said. "But as much as I yearned for the warm good food I was afraid of what else marriage might serve me."

Pa passed the lamb platter to me and I served myself a second helping and passed it to Simonakis who leapt on it eagerly.

"What are you afraid of?" Mrs. Bratsos asked him.

"The most terrible weapon of destruction since the invention of gunpowder," Simonakis said and with his fork speared a long and thick slice of meat. "The mouth of a nagging woman."

Pa laughed heartily and Marika and I smiled but Mrs. Bratsos looked grim.

"I am afraid, Mr. Simonakis," she said coldly. "Your values are in some disorder."

But Simonakis was busy digging into the lamb and made out he did not hear.

We all ate in silence for a bit, and I savored the tender meat. Pa poured more wine and Simonakis helped himself to a third helping.

Finally Mrs. Bratsos pushed up a strand of hair that had fallen across her forehead and drew a deep breath that swelled her huge bosom and dominated the table.

"It must be the church of the Annunciation," Mrs. Bratsos said firmly.

Everybody stopped eating for a moment and looked at her.

"The wedding," Mrs. Bratsos said. "I know your parish church here but it is a mess. The street is impossible. The Annunciation is across the street from the park and near the lake. It is lovely there."

I started to speak but Pa jumped first.

"What of Father Kontoyannis?" he asked and stared hard at Mrs. Bratsos.

Mrs. Bratsos shrugged. "Father Leontis will do just as well."

Marika watched her mother in silence. Even Simonakis had stopped eating. Pa shook his head, his face disturbed.

"I not consider any other church," he said. "In this parish we live all our lives."

"I do not like Father Leontis," Simonakis said. "He is a monarchist. Besides that he has asthma and whistles through his nose when he sings the service."

Mrs. Bratsos fixed him with a gimlet-eyed stare.

"You perhaps prefer your precious Father Konto-yannis? We have heard of that one even in Albuquerque. They say he is never more than a day ahead of being thrown out by the bishop. He disgraces the cloth."

"We will be married in St. Sophia," I said.

All four of them looked at me and the old lady was astounded. Simonakis nodded in emphatic agreement.

"This is our church," I said. "Our family has attended from the time we were children. If we were being married in Albuquerque the church would be your choice. But here we cannot marry in any other church."

Mrs. Bratsos cleared her throat wrathfully.

"Mama," Marika said. "It is foolish to argue. One church is like another. I would like to get married in their church."

The old lady silenced her with a baleful look.

"Kindly let me decide what is best for you," she said. "In gratitude for all I have done for you and all I have had to put up with, at least let me express my wishes."

"Express your wishes, Mama Bratsos," I said, "but we will be married in St. Sophia."

A stricken silence fell across the table. The old lady drew herself up as if she had been struck a mighty blow. Then something rumbled and it was Pa, his face all twisted to keep from laughing and the rumble was air escaping between his lips. Beside him Simonakis was grinning showing his great husked and yellowed teeth. The old lady glared furiously at both of them. Pa struggled mightily to compose himself and almost succeeded.

"You might show me courtesy, Angelo," Mrs. Bratsos said shrilly, "instead of sitting there choking. I would think you should be concerned I am not permitted to express my wishes at your table."

Pa sobered then and looked shamefaced. He glared at Simonakis who just as quickly stopped grinning.

"In my house, Stella," Pa explained patiently, "each man has right to speak mind. Angelo not run dictatorship."

"Long live freedom of speech!" Simonakis cried.

The old lady's voice lowered menacingly.

"I know how you run your house," she said. "One son married to an outsider and the other lacking courtesy to consider the wishes of his elders."

The reference to Mike made Pa's face darken. I felt angry and for Marika's sake tried to control myself. Pa stood up and without a word walked from the room into the parlor.

"Mama!" Marika said furiously. "You had no right to say that!"

The old lady did not answer but stood up and picked up an empty plate and swept out to the kitchen.

Simonakis looked grieved and pushed slightly away from the table.

"The lamb had too much grease," he said. "My stomach has become upset."

Marika smiled at me ruefully and started to clear the

dishes. Simonakis reached out and idly picked up an
olive and popped it into his mouth. Pa came back into
the room with his jaw set as hard as a rock.

"Please to sit down," he said gently to Marika. He
raised his voice. "Stella," he called. "Come back in
room."

He returned to his chair and sat down. Mrs. Bratsos
came to stand in the doorway.

"Please to sit down," Pa said. She did not move. Pa
fixed her with an ice-crowned glare and raised his voice.
"Please to sit down!"

She moved then, slightly flustered, and sat down.

"Now," Pa said. "Is not good we argue. Important
thing is for Marika and Tony be happy. Okay?"

Simonakis spit the pit of the olive into his hand and
nodded vigorously.

"Is not important what Mama think or what I think,"
Pa went on. "When young people marry first time, by
god, that time should not have old people tell how and
why."

"Angelo," the old lady tried to interrupt.

"Wait please," Pa said. "I have things I wish done.
You have things you wish done. You give up and I give
up and let young people decide own way."

"Bravo!" Simonakis said.

Pa scowled at him and stared back at the old lady.
She looked at him uneasily and turned to Marika to
seek support.

"I would like to express my wishes," she said plaintively. "May I not at least express my wishes?"

"Sure," Pa said and nodded firmly. "You are beloved mother and must express wishes. Young people must listen and think what you say."

"Mama Bratsos," I said and tried to sound sincere. "We love you. That counts for something too."

"Love is everything," Simonakis said fervently.

"Mama, please," Marika said.

The old lady hesitated and Pa was smiling and could really be a charmer, and then under the shadow of her ruffled plumes she forced a trace of a smile.

"As long as I am given respect," she said, and you could almost hear her caving in. "As long as I am allowed to express my wishes."

"You are beloved mother!" Pa said loudly, and he was generous in victory. "Must express wishes. Young people must listen carefully." He looked at me and then at Marika and shook his head and kept shaking it until we both joined him as if we were puppets on the same string.

"Peace on this noble house," Simonakis said grandly.

"Now we not worry for dishes," Pa said. "We all sit in parlor and good friend Simonakis goes home and brings Cretan lyre. This be good time for little Cretan music. We sing and dance Syrtos from Rethymnos."

"I will be pleased," Simonakis said gravely, "to play some love songs in honor of the young people."

"Let us do the dishes first," Mrs. Bratsos said trying to regain command. Pa waved her down and then with elaborate countesy ushered her and Marika into the parlor. He came back a moment later and peered around cautiously as if he was afraid the old lady had a microphone in the wall.

"Make care with old lady," he whispered to me. "Not smart let air from balloon all at once. Maybe blow up."

"What part of the homeland is she from?" Simonakis asked.

"Tegea," Pa answered.

Simonakis nodded soberly. "I understand now. That place is all rock. The women get tough and hard like mules."

"Your head is like mule," Pa whispered fiercely. "Shut big mouth or maybe old lady hear."

"Let her," Simonakis said and started for the back door to go for his lyre. "I have finished eating."

Pa threw up his hands in mute disgust and then we walked into the parlor.

Simonakis slammed the back door.

Chapter 10

IN A FEW MOMENTS SIMONAKIS HAD RETURNED AND
we all sat down in the parlor. I tugged Marika onto the
couch beside me. Simonakis held the curved lyre and
sat stiffly on a chair in a corner of the room and held
the small bow poised until we had quieted down.

"I play a love song first," he said gravely. "For the
young people."

He tapped a beat with his foot and drew the bow
across the strings in a sad and lingering wail. After a
moment he began to sing in a quavering voice.

> *"When I was young I loved a maiden*
> *With hair black like midnight.*
> *I loved her and left her.*
> *When I returned she was dead,*
> *Dead of a broken heart."*

Pa grimaced and waved his hand to stop the wail of the lyre.

"By god, you call that love song? Why not sing funeral moirologia and have done." He smiled cheerfully at Mrs. Bratsos who sat severely in her chair. "Make happy song so we can sing," he went on. "Angelo show off best voice in city, maybe in whole country." He winked at Marika.

Simonakis looked scornfully at Pa.

"You wish me to play," he said, "while you bellow like a sick bull and nobody can hear the music anyway. If you wish me to play, I will play, and you go sing in the alley."

"Let us all sing," I suggested, "and Pa will promise to sing quietly so the fine music of the lyre will be heard."

That pacified Simonakis slightly and he put the bow back to the lyre. He gave Pa one final warning look and began to play.

The sharp rhythm of a song about a winsome shepherdess of Pontos trilled about the room. Pa began by trying to sing in a subdued voice. I joined in and a moment later Marika began to sing softly. Mrs. Bratsos did not sing.

Pa sang a little louder and Simonakis glared at him and began to play more fiercely. But when Pa opened up he had a voice like a roaring mill furnace and after a moment more we could not hear the lyre. To reassert himself, Simonakis began to shriek. In another few bars he had locked Pa in a heated duet to drown him out and together they raised a deafening clamor.

Marika and I started laughing and had to stop singing. Mrs. Bratsos jumped out of her chair and waved vigorously for silence. Pa shut his mouth and the lyre died on a long thin wail.

"I have never heard such noise in my life," she said angrily. "You both must think you are in a coffeehouse with hoodlums. Now please to conduct yourselves more properly or Marika and I will leave the room."

Pa coughed and looked sheepish.

"Play Syrtos," he said to Simonakis. "You sing so poor maybe better we dance."

Simonakis glared at both Pa and Mrs. Bratsos and then snapped his lyre into place and swept the bow swiftly across the strings. Pa jumped into the center of the room and motioned to Marika.

"Come to dance," he said gaily. "Dance with Angelo."

Marika joined him and he took her hand and together they moved into the cadence of the dance. She followed his lead with her slender body nimble and graceful.

"Bravo!" Pa cried as he whirled. "Bravo, little peach, bravo!"

He was pleased and danced as a swift and agile giant, and holding his hand, Marika kept to the pace with her eyes bright and excited. This was the first time I had seen Marika dance and I was proud. Even Simonakis forgot his distemper and smiling broadly nodded his bald and brown old head in approval.

The doorbell must have rung once and we did not hear. When the music stopped it rang again, a long hard pealing that vibrated on and on.

"Who in hell ring like that?" Pa said angrily, and breathing hard from the dance he stamped out of the room to the door in the hall.

Marika came back to the couch, with her cheeks flushed and her hair tousled, and a crown of grace from the dance still ringed about her dark head.

"You were wonderful," I said softly. "You made me proud of you."

"I dance better than I cook," she whispered.

"After we are married," I said, "we will dance down to Walgreens for breakfast in the morning." She had to smile, and if her mother and Simonakis were not in the room I would have kissed her.

There was silence in the hall, and, wondering who had come in, I walked inside. Pa stood by the door with Father Kontoyannis.

"You're late, Father," I said. "You missed a dinner and a dance but we'll let you catch up." Then I saw his face tight with shadows hinged about the eyes. I looked at Pa and all his joy of the dance was gone and his cheeks dark and bruised.

"What's the matter?" I asked, and a cold and uneasy hand settled at my throat.

Pa turned and walked swiftly through the dining room into the kitchen.

"What's the matter, Father?" I asked again. "What is it?"

For another moment he did not answer. When he finally spoke his voice came low and troubled from his mouth.

"I have been with Mike," he said. "They have taken his wife to the hospital. Her time for birth has come premature. She had much pain and bleeding. They are concerned."

For a stricken instant all I could think was that now Pa knew about the baby. Then fear for Sheila and Mike flared in me as furious as a wind-swept fire.

I followed Pa into the kitchen. He stood by the table with his back to me and I did not dare break the oppressive silence until I heard Father Kontoyannis beside me.

"Pa," and I took a deep breath. "We better go to the hospital."

He turned with his body tense and his eyes black and glittering coals.

"I go first to hell," he said, and it came flaming from his lips.

"Angelo," the priest began.

Pa cut him off.

"Do not speak, Father," he said. "I feel this moment like I want die, like I want go deep in ground." He shook his head in bitter anger. "This is why he marry in midnight. After twenty-five years come like thief in night and spit on father. Now let him eat head."

I felt his anger and pain and yet nothing made sense but that Mike and Sheila needed us. I crossed the kitchen and got my jacket from the back of the door.

"Which hospital, Father?" I asked and tried not to look at Pa.

"The Carrada," he said. "Across from the Lutheran church."

I ran most of the four blocks to the hospital and when I reached the old building I was winded.

For a moment at the desk before the stiff-faced gray haired woman I could not manage breath to speak. When I asked for Sheila's room she told me no visitors were allowed. I explained my brother was upstairs and that our priest had called the family. She sent me to the elevator where an old bald man with puffy eyes and a mark of death on his powdery cheeks waited and closed the door. When I got out on the fifth floor, I saw Mike almost at once.

He was sitting alone in a single-windowed alcove at the end of the long empty corridor. I started toward him and the doors of some rooms were open and silent watchful faces in white-sheeted beds turned soundlessly and marked my passing. In one room a man lay with a tube in his nose and a tank beside his bed and a hissing as of life leaving the flesh. Only he did not turn as I passed but stared in some hopeless and terrible way at the ceiling.

Mike was in his mill clothes, the dark and frayed woolen shirt and khaki pants and steel-toed shoes. Close to him I saw the confusion and dark grief that laced his cheeks.

"Mike," I said. "How is she?"

He parted his lips to speak and then swallowed as if his tongue and throat were dry.

"Upstairs for more than three hours now," he said. He shook his head slowly, wretchedly from side to side. "She went to bed to rest in the afternoon when I left for the mill. She woke with bad cramps and a lot of bleeding. The old lady downstairs was at the store and nobody heard Sheila hollering and calling for help for quite a while. She was bleeding so bad she was afraid to try and come down the stairs. They called me and I got home the same time as the ambulance."

Thinking of Sheila bleeding and screaming alone chilled my flesh.

"It's not time for the baby yet, is it?" I said.

"It's not time," he said. "It's not nearly time. The doc says maybe a miscarriage will be the worst, but she bled a lot, and we got to wait and see. We just got to wait."

He looked at his hands on his knees. Out of nowhere a nurse appeared in the corridor, walking soundlessly and moving like some kind of white clothed wraith out of one room into another.

The disorder in Mike seemed to spread to my body. I spoke, as desperate to assure myself as to comfort him.

"She'll be all right. Mike, don't worry, because she'll be all right."

"Are you sure she's going to be all right? Are you sure?"

Something about the way he asked, grimly, tenaciously shaking the words the way a dog shakes a piece of meat. Then the violence went out of him and he leaned his arms wearily against the wood of his chair.

"Why don't the old man come?"

"Maybe soon," I said, and the lie bitter off my tongue.

He stood up then, big-boned and strong-faced as Pa, and looked down the silent corridor. He turned and walked to the window and stared into the darkness.

"You're a liar," he said quietly. "A goddam liar. The old man isn't coming. He don't care."

The silence returned and burdened me as a weight upon my back. Only the hissing of air in the room with the tank could be faintly heard.

"Mike, he does care. He does care."

From the window he came restlessly back to the chair. His hands moved uncertainly and clasped fingers across his stomach.

"Maybe he's right," he said. "Maybe he knows now we did wrong and got to be punished. Maybe he stays away because that's the way it's got to be."

He rose again and walked down the hall, his heavy shoes scuffing upon the floor and the shadows of his long body sweeping along the wall. By the drinking fountain he bent and drank and straightened up and wiped his mouth with the back of his hand and returned without looking into the rooms he passed.

I could not help myself and thought of death. I could feel it in the empty corridor with the walls stark as the hewn stone of tombs, in the silence of the rooms where the watchful faces waited, and in the fear on Mike's face.

"I never told you," he said. "I never told you how many men I killed in the war." He paused and his eyes were terrible to see. "I killed with a gun and with grenades. Once I even killed with a knife. His blood got all over me."

"Mike, in war everybody has to kill. They would have killed you."

He waved my words aside and his mouth twisted.

"You're just a punk kid. You don't understand how a guy gets covered with blood. You can't wash it off or

wipe it away. It gets on your hands and after that anything you touch runs with blood. That's why the old
man won't come."

"Mike, no," I said helplessly. "He will come soon. I
know he has to come soon."

But I knew Pa was not coming. And knowing that
made me helpless and afraid.

A nurse came and took him to the elevator and he
did not look back. A red light flashed outside one of the
rooms as if it was a mute cry on the stillness. The nurse
rose from the desk and walked to the room and left me
alone.

I had to go home and get Pa. Somehow I had to bring
him back.

I left the hospital. I walked the late evening streets
past the taverns and coffeehouses full of smoke and old
men sitting indolently at tables inside the windows. In
the distance the mournful wail of a crane whistle in the
mill. I shivered and passed the mouth of a dark and
hidden alley and a gust of wind swept about my ears,
bringing a strange and restless remembering of things
past.

I entered the house and walked to the parlor and they
all sat waiting, all but Pa.

Marika came to me with Father Kontoyannis close
behind her.

"How is she?" Marika asked and her eyes troubled
and her voice uneven with concern, but she could not

really know. None of them could understand the way it was.

"They wouldn't let us see her," I said. "I left Mike alone."

Mrs. Bratsos clucked her tongue. Simonakis stared at me gravely. I looked at the priest.

"Where is Pa?"

He motioned slowly upstairs and tried to take my arm.

"Mike needs him, Father," I said. "He wants Pa to come. I got to talk to Pa."

"Shall I go again?" he asked, and I guess of all outside the family he did understand. "Perhaps you and I could return to the hospital together."

His voice pleading a little as if to find an answer that would keep me from Pa.

"Mike wants Pa," I said. "He just wants Pa."

I turned and went quickly up the stairs. I walked into Ma's room without knocking. Pa sat on the edge of the bed staring at the floor and looked up startled.

"Pa," I said, and tried to speak quietly. "You got to go to the hospital. Mike needs you."

"Angelo," and the priest had come silently into the room behind me and closed the door. "Angelo, the girl may die. They may lose the baby."

Pa rose angrily off the bed.

"Is too late now," he said. "Now let girl burn for

what she do to family. Bring shame and hate on my house. Let girl burn."

"Pa," I said. "Pa, who are you? Are you God you got a right to say who has to burn. You think you're God to send people to hell?"

"I not go!" he said fiercely. "I swear by my dead I not go. Let son and girl he take in shame burn, but I swear by my dead I not go."

"Angelo," the priest's voice pleaded. "Do not deliver your son into the hands of spoilers. Do not answer burn with burn and wound with wound."

Pa raised one clenched fist and brought it down hard across the post of the bed. His flesh made a heavy slamming sound against the wood.

"Let me this room in peace," he said hoarsely. "By god, let me in peace."

"If you do not go, Angelo," the priest went on relentlessly, "you will never know peace again."

Then the dark fury burst in Pa's face.

"Goddam you," he said to the priest. "Goddam you for come my house and spit my face of sin. Goddam priest who stand before church, before God, and spit own sin. Who sneak at night like dog to bed of woman. Come now my house and spit my face of sin. Goddam you wash own sin first."

The priest came beside me and stood before Pa. His face was naked, more naked than the face of any man

I had ever seen, the face of Abel before the rock of Cain.

"Yes, I go to a woman," he said, and the words were low and spaced but each one trembled, as if it was born upon some overwhelming pain. "I go to a gentle widow who asks nothing of me and we lie together in the dark. Most of the time there is little I can do but sometimes I play the part of a man, feebly and without great clashing of cymbals, and afterwards I sleep and feel less alone." He paused and drew breath. "I drink, Angelo, and I carouse, Angelo, and now you know I am not like Jesus, I do not turn the other cheek."

Pa's body towered over the body of the priest, and still in some strange and indefinable way they were become of one size. The priest in smoke and fire and vengeful as the mad God on the ceiling of the church.

"A long time has passed," the priest said and his eyes held Pa's face like teeth. "But can you remember why you built a hallowed room to a dead wife, why in the name of love you created a shrine to sit in like God, curtained from mortal men, and to hell with everything that lives and breathes and walks but Angelo, mighty Angelo."

"You talk crazy," Pa said, and all anger was drained from his face and fear rising on the flesh of his cheeks.

"Am I crazy, Angelo?" the priest said and his voice was low. "If I am crazy then all I remember did not really pass. If I am crazy then this moment is a dream and so was the Sicilian woman with the head of Medusa and hair like serpents who was your burning love and could not be shared. If I am crazy there was never a day in April long ago when you almost killed the charger, Komarski, because he sought to take her from you. If I am crazy then all the other women were not real, all the great wild and driven whores with frenzy to match your own, and all the drinking and fighting was not real, and all the times I pleaded with Cacha at the station to help in charges brought against you by men whose bones you had broken with your fists."

I tried to think but the words tangled about my head. I tried to bring reason and sense to what the priest was saying but nothing was clear.

"And this you thought your wife never knew," the priest said. "You thought everything aside from a few bruises and a few nights of drinking could be concealed from her. But she cried to me what she never spoke of to you. In the dark confessional she cried of her desolate nights with the small sons asleep, while you rumbled your hours with the great Medusa tart. In the end when incurable illness came to her, you sat beside her bed and held her hand and tried to drive strength back into her body to keep her alive and to free yourself of guilt and shame, but it was too late. In silence she died and like a great stricken Judas you fought to raise your sons with all the mighty affection you had denied her." His voice fell to a dark and burdened whisper. "You destroyed then, and now in fury you will destroy again."

I remember Pa's face at that moment. I will never forget what he looked like then, his strength gone, his body scarred and his eyes cold and dead and alone.

Chapter 11

I LEFT THE ROOM. I WALKED DOWN THE STAIRS AND left the house. The street was dark but for the lights glistening in bowls above the gutters. A wind rank with the smell of the river touched my face.

If we can know the day, the hour or the moment that a period in our lives comes to an end, the day, the hour or the fleeting moment when there is an end and before a beginning, I knew my time then.

A time of bitterness and growing anger. A strange and savage moment when I seemed lost and uprooted.

In the lobby of the hospital I found Mike. He was sitting in a far corner along the wall.

I sat down beside him and when he turned to look at me the wildness that had been in his face earlier was shadowed by weariness.

"They brought Sheila to her room," he said and he spoke so quietly I had to bend close to hear. "She is sleeping. They think she will be all right."

"What about the baby?" I asked, and even before he answered I knew the way it must be for the sins of the fathers visited upon the sons.

"It was too small," he said in that quiet and terrible voice. "It had no strength. A crippled, twisted boy, dead when they pulled it out."

Then the fury swept my flesh again and I remembered Pa, arrogant and uncaring in his anger, condemning as if his hand was the hand of some vengeful god.

"It wasn't your fault," I said. "Not your fault or Sheila's. It was his fault. The sins were his and the blood was his."

I did not care about anything but to release some of the bitterness that choked me and I told him. I told him all the priest had said, of the nights and the tears and the desecrations. Of how she knew and sat in the dark confessional and cried of the way it was.

When I had finished, as if the words burning off my tongue had heat to draw graven images out of darkness, the door of the lobby opened and Pa walked in.

He must have seen Mike and me at almost the same instant we saw him. For a long moment none of us moved. He wore no coat and was bare-headed and his face twisted under strips of shadow and light.

You are too late, I said, and only my tongue formed

words and no sound passed my lips and he came slowly across the lobby.

"You are too late," I said, and he was still too far away to hear. He came closer, and as if he lacked courage to bridge the last few steps he stopped a short distance away. Close enough for me to bear witness to his scarred cheeks.

"You are too late," I said. "They don't need you now. The baby is dead."

"Goddam you," Mike said softly. "Goddam you butcher. Goddam you."

Pa just stood there. He made no sound and you could almost feel his breath choked off in his throat. Then he turned and walked to the door.

I stayed with Mike for a long time. We did not speak and the only sound was the occasional buzz of the phone and the voice of the woman in answer. Once or twice patients were admitted, a child being carried by his parent, a pregnant woman slow and heavy at her husband's side.

There was nothing we could do and yet we waited, and to banish the cold I thought of Marika. I must have slept, because a feverish dream snapped me awake.

I could not sit and wait any more. I left Mike alone and walked into the darkness.

It was the quiet folded hours after midnight and most of the city asleep. The streets stretched a maze of paths among the darkened houses and I walked alone.

I did not walk with plan or purpose but something brought me to Gerontis'. The door was locked but there was light inside. I knocked and after a few moments knocked again. Gerontis' face appeared and I called my name and he unlocked the door.

"You look for your father," Gerontis said, and he shook his head. He motioned to the back. "He is here. He is here."

I walked through the big shadowed room and most of the tables were empty but here and there some old man lay asleep with his head cradled in his arms. One dreamed fitfully and moaned and another coughed and a third sat and started at nothing.

At a table in the back I found Pa and Simonakis. Pa with his head cradled on the table between his hands. Simonakis sat stiff and upright as if keeping silent vigil over the table.

I pulled up a chair and sat down. The smell of masticha was heavy about our heads.

"He has drunk all night," Simonakis said. "He would not stop."

"Mike's baby died," I said.

"I know," Simonakis said. "All night he has spoken of the dead."

Then Pa cried out. He raised his head and caught his breath. He saw me and for a moment drew back as if he thought me part of his fevered dream.

"Why in hell you sit this table?" he asked, his voice harsh and thick. "Why you not leave me alone? Why you sit like goddam hawk and bite my eyes?"

"Angelo," Simonakis said and he spoke softly as you console a child.

Pa fumbled with the bottles on the table.

"More wine!" he shouted loudly, and his voice rang brokenly in the big still room. "More wine!"

"You have had enough, Angelo," Simonakis said and he gently touched Pa's arm. "Gerontis is closed. He cleans up to go home."

Pa did not seem to hear and looked helplessly at his hands around the empty bottles. His eyes hollowed in shadows and the furies about his head.

"Why in hell you not leave," he said again and his voice low and trembling. "Why in hell you sit my table?"

Simonakis spoke softly and soothingly, but Pa shook him off.

"Do not worry for me," he said defiantly. "I am Angelo Varinakis and I am lion and I am not afraid. I am Angelo and I make steel like Joe Magarac."

"Yes," Simonakis shook his head in brusque agreement. "You are Big Angelo and as great as Magarac."

Pa shook one of the bottles to see if there was anything left and then pushed it furiously away.

"Do you remember night my crew roll record?" Pa said and now he spoke loudly and a few old men at

211

other tables sat up and listened. "Night when slabs come like bullets from furnace. When overhead crane fly like great bird."

At a nearby table a man stood up, a sharp-faced old man, still lean as a cypress and waved his glass jubilantly in the air.

"I was there on that night, Angelo," he said. "Your voice was the thunder. You made giants of your men. I tell of that night to my children and they will tell their children after them."

An old man near the bar rose and he was white haired and I could not clearly see his face. He raised his arms that were gnarled like the misshapen branches of an ancient tree bent with the mark of death, and he chanted Pa's name.

"Angelo," the old man called out in a quavering voice. "Angelo, Angelo, mighty Angelo."

Pa lurched from his chair and with furious force hurled an empty bottle across the room high against a wall where it cracked and shattered.

"I am Big Angelo!" Pa bellowed and his voice roared thick and hoarse with wine and power. "I am lion and not need any man. I not fear any man. I am Big Angelo and I walk earth alone!"

When he finished the old men answered. They chanted his name and their shrill cries of acclaim echoed strangely in the room. One shouted wildly and another shrieked and a third pounded the table with his fist.

Then the voices faded and fell away and the old man lean as a cypress was the last to stop and still pounded the table after the rest were quiet, and then he too gave up.

Pa looked down to me. He raised one hand as if to shield his eyes and twisted from the table and started to the door.

Simonakis jumped from his chair as if to follow and took a few stiff steps and stopped and looked helplessly back at me. I got up and followed Pa to the street.

Outside the coffeehouse the night air was chilled and the city silent. Over the mill buildings the sky burned. At the corner for just a moment I saw Pa unsteady through the beam of a streetlamp and then lost him again.

I followed him walking quickly until I crossed the street and when I saw him I slowed down. He was almost half a block ahead of me swaying close to the wall of closed stores. When he bumped the wall he paused to brace himself and then pushed off.

By the time he reached our street he was using his arms as great paddles to propel himself forward and keep himself on his feet. I could hear his harsh and labored breathing across the darkness. When he reached our house he pushed open the gate to the yard and staggered to the front door.

I crossed the street and waited by the gate. He had found his key and was trying to insert it in the door.

For a long time he tried to fit the lock. Then wearily he rested. A car passed and the beams of light shook him again into motion. After a few moments he gave up, his arms limp at his sides, his chest against the frame.

Then from the slab mill beyond our street sounded the long thin wail of the flying crane, as if in some nameless way it was coming to Pa's aid. I saw him stiffen and heard him violent against the wood and then the door opened.

He went straight for the stairs and when I entered the house he had made it to the top of the landing. I followed him and in the hall outside the bedrooms I saw Marika and her mother. They were both in robes and standing close to the wall as if frozen by Pa's entrance. Marika's face was pale and pinched with concern and her mother's face was dark and impassive. I looked at Marika and made a mute gesture of consolation with my fingers and my lips and then followed Pa to the door of Ma's room. The room was hollowed in darkness but I heard his uneven breathing. I stepped inside and closed the door.

Pa was on his knees beside the bed, his arms extended upon the sheets. His hands groped along the cloth and fumbled toward the pillows at the head. And something about the slow stiff way he seemed to be searching with his fingers chilled my flesh.

He whispered then with his voice lost on the darkness

and he clutched and stroked the cloth. He whispered again, his voice that of an old man with all bravado gone and all brittle and arrogant courage disappeared. I did not want to hear because I knew he was whispering to Ma, and the restless groping fingers reaching to her, in some way trying to make her hear and understand.

I went to the bed and knelt beside him and shook him by the shoulders gently to let him know I was there.

"Pa," I said. "It's all right. Pa, I love you. I love you."

He twisted to me and whispered my name and with his cold fingers touched my lips and the hot tears came burning to my eyes and the blind tears ran wet on his own cheeks.

Chapter 12

JUNE IS THE LONG DAY OF THE SUN. THE LIGHT OF dawn comes moist and early. In our yard the tall yellow sunflowers bloom beside the stones.

In the vacant lots under the shadow of the great dark mills the children scream as they play. On the trees before the drab frame houses the leaves of summer toss in the warm winds.

June is the long evening of the twilight. The moths wake in the dusk and flutter about the glistening street-lamps. The rumblings of the mill sound sharp and clear. As the last torn streaks of sun fade beyond the roofs of the city, the crickets hidden in the weeds begin their shrill chirp.

In June I was graduated from college. I wore a black cap and gown and stood with a hundred other seniors in the domed and cavernous chapel with the sun misting through the stained-glass windows. When my name was called I came forward and accepted my degree. All the time Pa sat in the crowd and when it was over he hugged me silently and held the diploma with incredible reverence. Mike and Sheila were there, but they sat apart from Pa.

Mike had not forgiven Pa. He had not entered our house since that night in April. Sheila tried to bring them together, but Mike's wound ran deep and all he could remember was blood and his dead son and how Pa came too late. Pa remembered too.

In that month, too, Mr. and Mrs. Bratsos brought Marika from Albuquerque for our marriage.

The night before the wedding I could not sleep and tossed fitfully for hours after going to bed. The women baking in the kitchen under the whip-lash tongue and stiff finger of Mrs. Bratsos rumbled until early in the hours after midnight. I must have fallen asleep for a while, and when I woke, the house was quiet and a faint trace of dawn glistened through the curtain at the window.

I felt wide awake and left my bed. I walked quietly down the hall past the rooms in which Marika and her parents slept. I wondered if she were awake and her night as restless as mine.

The kitchen door was slightly ajar and I thought one of the women had left it open. I started to close it and saw Pa in his bathrobe sitting in a corner of the porch.

"Pa," I said. "Couldn't you sleep?"

He shook his head and spoke softly.

"I come downstairs to watch first light," he said.

We stood silent and listened. A stillness across the city as if the earth was holding its breath. A strange unreal moment with the vast sky of night suspended for a moment between darkness and light.

"Pa," I said. "Jesus, Pa, I'm getting married today."

He had to laugh softly.

"By god, boy," he said. "I know. I know."

"But married, Pa," I said. "No joke."

"No joke," he said and there was a sadness in his voice.

I leaned my hands across the chilled railing. An early breeze barely moved the silent air.

"I guess the way it has to be," I said. "First one generation and then another. Your marriage day and now mine and someday that of my sons."

He moved forward in his chair and it drew his face from shadow into the cold faint light.

"I sit here and think," he said. "Of things fathers pass to sons. Money or wisdom — what is damn word?"

"Legacy, Pa?"

"Right, legacy," he said. "I think what goddam legacy I give to you. What you have from me after twenty years in my house."

I went and sat beside him and the light misted his

218

cheeks and his eyes were hollowed and hidden. I remembered many things and marked the strange way his
big hands folded in resignation on his knees.

"I not talk of money or property," he said. "I talk of
things, important things father can pass to son." He
opened his hands and slowly closed them again. "I give
you nothing."

His face was so close to me I could have reached out
and touched the cheeks so weary in the faint growing
light. And he stared beyond the roofs of the dark houses
at the changing sky.

"You make a mistake, Pa," I said. "You think when
you die, when the old country people die, that your
faith dies with you. Pa, that isn't true. Won't your faith
live on in me and in my sons? Maybe that is your legacy,
Pa, your faith going into the next generation."

He did not answer and the light grew stronger. The
buildings loomed more darkly against the brightening
sky. Up the alley a morning paper boy pulled a creaking
wagon.

There was noise in our kitchen and a moment later,
with her hair unkempt and her cheeks puffed from
sleep, Mrs. Bratsos stuck her head out the door.

"It is good you are both up early," she said loudly.
"There are a hundred things that must be done. A hundred things. This wedding will be a disgrace. If I did
not take hold they would not get done. Tony must not
see Marika before the wedding. Hurry and dress so you

can help. Hurry." She snapped her head back into the kitchen and closed the door.

Pa rose heavily from his chair and helplessly made a face.

"My beloved mother-in-law," I said. "I am doomed."

"Up early in morning like hawk," Pa said. "Even before cock crows."

He stopped beside me and hesitantly touched my arm.

"Mike will come to wedding?" he said. "Sure he will come with Sheila?"

"They will come, Pa," I said. "We rented our tuxedos from the same place. He will come."

"He must come," he said. "Is bad luck on wedding if he does not come."

"He will come, Pa," I said.

He turned to look one last time at the morning and at the sunflowers in our yard. He stood for a long silent moment.

"Where?" he said, and his voice hung wondering on the stillness. "Where are years that have gone? Where?"

Later that day when we left the house for the church, Pa and Simonakis and I rode in Barut's car. Of all of us, Simonakis looked most resplendent in a tuxedo that must have been styled by Custer's tailor during the Indian Wars. But he wore it with great dignity. The rest of us did not fare as well. Pa's tuxedo was too small for his broad bulky body and mine was a shade too big and Barut was a cave man in a bow tie.

We made one stop to pick up my godfather, Falcounis, who was going to be our best man. He was an old man who had known my family for many years and as a child I remembered with delight the sweet rich taste of his homemade chocolates.

While Pa went in to get him, a few children playing on the street clustered about the car and watched us through the windows with awed and curious faces.

"They think we are undertakers," I said. "They wonder who is dead."

Simonakis made a fierce face and they scattered. Pa came out holding the old godfather by the arm.

Before the church we unloaded. Barut jumped out and came around and opened my door with a grin and a flourish. The car bringing Marika and her parents had already arrived and she was inside. A church trustee came down the stairs quickly to greet us and speaking loudly led us up the stairs. Men and women stared and smiled as we passed and I was proud and flustered and felt myself a bull in a field, or a cock on a walk.

In the narthex of the church I saw Mike and Sheila. He was in his tux, tall and lean, and for a moment he smiled and I thought he was coming over, but Pa was beside me and Mike turned away. Pa walked past me silently into the church.

They walked to me then and Sheila appeared bright and excited.

"Tony," she said. "Tony, Marika is beautiful."

I felt my heart beating hard.

"Do I look all right?" I asked. "This damn suit doesn't fit. I told that damn tailor it was too big. Is it too bad?"

"You look great, kid," Mike said, and he brushed a speck of dust from my lapel.

"Your father looks fine too," Sheila said. "Doesn't he, Mike?"

Mike nodded and did not speak.

The trustee motioned me to come. I turned to them both one last time.

"Stay close," I said. "Just stay close."

"Sure," Mike grinned. "We'll be right with you all the way to the wedding bed if you like."

"Not that close," I said.

In the front of the church I stood flanked by Simonakis and Falcounis. Behind us the long center aisle of the church was covered with a carpet of white cloth and lined with great green palms. A small table had been placed before us holding the trays with the rings and with the wreaths of waxed orange blossoms. At either side of the altar was a large satin-ribboned candle as tall as a man.

By carefully turning my head I could see the

222

church full of men and women. Sheila and Mike and Barut and Pa in a front pew and not together but with space left between them for Mr. and Mrs. Bratsos who were still with Marika in the foyer of the church.

Father Kontoyannis came through the portals of the iconostasis and stood before the table. He wore a gold brocaded robe in layers of golden cloth and sash and cord.

If all of us had changed in some way since that night in April, on none of us was that change so grievously evident as it was on the priest. As if a part of his tempered spirit had fled, as if all the reason that guided his days had paced him into disorder. He performed his duties and ministered to his congregation, but men and women spoke of him in whispers and hinted darkly of some nameless retribution.

Pa and the priest had been close, as close as men could be, and they had turned on one another. They knew the vulnerability of one another's flesh and this let them strike deep. In the presence of one another each must have been reminded of his defection, and each must have felt his guilt. I could not bear to see them together.

From one of the doors at the side of the altar the plump little deacon from Albuquerque emerged and came to stand beside the priest. He had rosy cheeks and a dapper mustache.

The organ began. A rich deep swelling of sound that ran through the marrow of my bones.

A stir of whispering rose from the men and women. I twisted my head warily and down the center aisle a bridesmaid carried an armful of pink roses. A few steps behind her another bridesmaid, the eldest daughter of Mrs. Lanaras. Then in a festive and abundantly petticoated little dress the child who was the youngest daughter of Mrs. Lanaras, strewing petals of flowers as if she were a tiny nymph performing the rites of spring.

Marika entered the church on the arm of her father.

I shut my eyes for a moment listening to the deep rolling tones of the organ and imagined her coming closer and counted the beat for their steps. When I opened my eyes again she had reached the small stairway before the altar. She was all loveliness in white, and through the sheer veil her eyes and lips gleamed. Falcounis nudged me and I remembered and walked the few steps between us and took her from her father and kissed his hand and brought her back before the table.

"Blessed are all they that fear the Lord," Father Kontoyannis said and his resonant voice rang through the silent church. The black robed choirmaster answered. "Glory to Thee, O our God, Glory to Thee."

"And walk in his ways," the priest said.

"Glory to Thee, O our God, Glory to Thee."

"Blessed be the Kingdom of the Father and of the

Son and of the Holy Ghost, now and forever and from all ages to all ages."

"Amen," the choirmaster said.

For the first time the deacon spoke in a shrill voice that fitted his rosy cheeks. While he chanted he looked profoundly up to God.

"In peace let us beseech the Lord."

"Lord have mercy," the choirmaster sang.

Father Kontoyannis stepped forward and raised one long sleeved arm and the cloth of his robe fell back and exposed the thin and tendoned wrist, reminiscent of that Sunday of revelation.

"O God most holy and maker of all creation, who through thy love to man didst change the rib of our forefather Adam into woman and didst bless both and say increase and multiply and have dominion over the earth, and didst make of them one flesh, for which cause a man shall leave his father and his mother and shall cleave unto his wife and they two shall be one flesh."

In the silent church the men and women listened and perhaps remembered their own unions and an old woman cried. Outside in the still gray sky that threatened rain a bird passed and trailed its throaty call.

"Remember them, O Lord our God, as thou didst remember thy forty Holy Martyrs, sending down upon them crowns from heaven. Remember them, O God, who are come together in this joy. Remember, O Lord our God, thy servants and bless them."

The old woman still cried, her tears falling among the fragrant petals of the roses beside the flickering candles.

"Grant them of the fruit of their bodies, O Lord, exalt them like the cedars of Lebanon, like a luxuriant vine. Give them seed in number like unto the full ears of grain. Let them behold their children's children like a newly planted olive-orchard round about their table, that they may shine like the stars of heaven in thee, our God."

Marika and Tony. Tony and Marika. And for this cause, the priest had said, a man shall leave his father and his mother and shall cleave unto his wife and they two shall be one flesh.

Father Kontoyannis raised the wreaths of blossoms placing one upon my head.

"The servant of God, Anthony, is crowned . . ."

The other wreath over Marika's head, flowers gleaming vividly above the white fold of her veil.

". . . for the servant of God, Marika."

He stepped forward and three times exchanged the wreaths on our heads and three times chanted the blessing and three times made the sign of the cross.

We exchanged the rings and drank from the common cup and he led us three times in a circle about the table before the altar. Falcounis came behind straining on his toes to hold the wreaths upon our heads.

The priest raised his hand in the sign of the cross, his face in that moment strangely fluid and sustained between candles and flowers.

"In the name of the Father, and of the Son, and of the Holy Ghost, Amen."

"Amen," the choirmaster said. He closed the book and snapped off the small light above the stand.

I turned to Marika. Her lashes were dark and her throat rose pleasingly from the collar of her gown and in that moment her face was that of a child between dreaming and waking.

I kissed her and a murmur of voices and laughter rippled through the church. Father Kontoyannis took our hands in his own.

"God bless you both," he said softly in a way that seemed to come from deep inside him and he held our hands for a long time. Until behind him the little deacon cleared his throat and smiled showing small sharp white teeth and shook our hands with vigor. Then the choirmaster in his formless black gown brushed our hands in passing.

Old Falcounis stood on his toes and kissed our cheeks and I smelled the scents of chocolate as if over the years the odor of the sweet rich creams had pervaded his flesh.

Pa came and Sheila and Mike and Mr. and Mrs. Brat-

sos and Simonakis and Barut and all the others. Pa
hugged us wordlessly and rubbed his nose hard. Mrs.
Bratsos smothered us to her great bosom and wept great
fountains of tears.

Afterwards the old women filed by and kissed our
hands for good fortune and stained our cheeks with the
tears old women weep at weddings. The old men passed
and shook our hands and mumbled greetings and their
faces scarred and leathery from age and the heat of the
mills. Dark haired girls giggled and dark haired youths
strutted and children pulled at their mothers' skirts.

Until the last of the congratulations were over and
our cheeks given a chance to dry.

In the hall downstairs, two long wooden tables were
set along the walls and covered with freshly laundered
and still drab cloths that had seen hundreds of recep-
tions. On the tables were great platters of lamb and
rings of crisp-crusted bread and squares of moist cheese
and decanters of dark red wine.

In a few moments the tables were full and the plump
little deacon raised his hand for silence and in a brisk
voice said grace. Afterwards the sounds of metal and
glass and people eating swept the hall as furious as
thunder. Gerontis and his fleet-footed waiters raced
from place to place filling glasses with wine as quickly
as they were emptied. Falcounis, his cheeks flushed
with pleasure, waved to old friends and between

mouthfuls of lamb tried to explain to me the art of making chocolates. A few seats down the table I could see the mighty bosom of Mrs. Bratsos almost in her plate. The wine warmed me and I looked with elation upon the noisy brimming tables.

At the end of our table a young man dreamed over his wine and beside him a well-fed old man lit a long cigar. Two girls in bright dresses passed and giggled to us in greeting. A film of smoke rose from the tables and Gerontis came arm in arm with Simonakis to drink for the fifth time to our health.

Then a sudden riotous clapping and stamping of feet began. Stahakis and his three piece band were ascending the platform at the end of the hall. They adjusted their chairs and their legs and tuned their instruments. Men and women and children hushed in expectation. A moment later the music began. Faintly first, as they gathered power, then swelling into the sharp lilting rhythms of the dance.

Falcounis rose unsteadily and gestured grandly to Marika and myself. The custom of the Koumbaros to dance the bride and groom. I took Marika by the hand and followed him apprehensively to the center of the room. He motioned us into line behind him and Marika held the hem of her gown and stood between us. He raised one arm slowly, flexing it to loosen the muscles and stir up circulation, and did the same with one leg and then the other. Then he arched back his head and looked arrogantly at the ceiling. From deep inside him, buried under layers of age and memory, came a bold shrill shout, the cry of the Greek bridging two thousand years. The music flamed and he stamped his brittle legs in the dance and we followed.

We danced again and again. Others joined the line and stamped and circled. Pa led the dance proudly for his son and new daughter. I led the dance, wild and turbulent and hot with wine, and Mike holding behind me. Marika led the dance, graceful and serene, and the room quiet with awe. Mrs. Bratsos led the dance, pacing the line slowly and somberly, while the sweat poured down her cheeks. After a while old Falcounis danced again, held up on either side by younger men.

A moment came when I had my fill of wine and music. I looked at Marika sitting beside me and something caught tightly in my flesh. I motioned to Mike, who was going to drive us to the hotel across the city, and he went to get the car.

Sheila and Marika and I left the hall and the dancers whirled, and Simonakis, red-faced and howling, led the line and few must have seen us go. We walked the shadowed corridor and up the stairs to the rooms at the rear of the church where we had left our clothes. Sheila helped Marika change in one room and I changed in another and neatly folded the tux in the box for Mike to return. When I finished they were not yet ready and I walked into the dark church.

Silent and shadowed now but for a few flickering candles and quiet after the festive hall. The palms loomed like great winged birds in the dusk and the scent of incense and fragrance of roses still hung on the air.

I walked toward the altar, my feet soundless upon the soiled white cloth. There was a light under the door of the small room to the side. I knew it must be Father Kontoyannis, and after an instant of hesitation I walked to the door and knocked.

When he answered I walked in. He was sitting at a small table sorting through papers. He had changed from the golden robe to a dark suit and the white collar about his throat. He smiled and nodded greeting.

"We are leaving, Father," I said. "I wanted to say good-by because we will be gone from the city a couple of weeks."

He stood up and slowly offered me his hand.

"I think this may be a final good-by," he said quietly. "Your wedding is the last service I will hold in my church. Next week a new priest will assume this parish."

"Why, Father?" I asked. "Why?"

For a long moment he did not answer, as if he were searching for a way to speak the words he wanted to say.

"I am tired, Tony," he said. "I am suddenly more tired than I have ever been before." He looked down at his hands. "There is a monastery on the side of Lania, the mountain of many sheep, not far from where I was born. As children we could hear the bell in the tower calling the monks to meals and to prayers at twilight. Sometimes on clear days in that time of year you could see them planting and tilling in their small plots on the side of the mountain. I have written and obtained permission to take their vows and enter their order and remain with them as long as I live."

He stared at me for a long moment. He clasped his hands in some harried joining of his fingers.

"That is not all," he said. "That is not the only reason I am leaving." He shook his head with despair across his cheeks and in his eyes. "I leave because I have lost faith in myself. I can no longer smile and weep with one face. I am forsaken of the Father and I am tired and I turn my face to Jerusalem."

His voice trailed off into silence. He looked down to his hands.

"Go, Tony," he said. "Go to your new bride."

I spoke slowly and clearly.

"I will miss you, Father," I said. "I will think of you often and I will miss you."

We faced one another and he seemed to want to say something else but shook his head numbly and held silent. I turned and left the room.

Marika was waiting in the foyer of the church with Sheila. We walked to the side door and in the alcove

Pa waited to tell us good-by. Suddenly I was grateful for the shadows.

"Time to leave," he said huskily. "You go now."

He kissed Marika tenderly and touched her cheek gently with his hand. He turned to me. I think he wanted to kiss me and was uncertain of my new manhood, and beside Sheila and Marika I could not think of the words to tell him it was all right. He reached for my arm and his other hand gripped my shoulder and he held me that way for what seemed a long time. Then he let me go and we went out the door to the street where Mike waited in the car.

The night was dark, without stars, and from somewhere far off came the scent of rain. Marika and I got in back and Sheila in front with Mike.

I looked back once as we pulled away and saw the great shadowed block of his body in the doorway. In that fleeting moment I thought of all the things I might have said.

Much later in the hotel Marika and I lay together in bed in a large room shadowed but for a dim night lamp in a corner. There were long curtains on the windows and behind them shades that rustled slightly against the open sash. Far out in the warm moist night, thunder rumbled and split the sky. I turned on my side and looked again at Marika.

We had loved for the first time and in looking at her

nakedness I relived again the wonder of our loving. Her body in that phase of lamplight unbelievably soft and pale. Her breasts small, of dark nippled delicacy for loving. Her slender thighs still and languid now and only a while before so supple and fiery beneath mine.

How far from death, how close to pain, the first sweet savage joining of our bodies. Her fingers tight across my back, her throat trembling with the long end of the spasm of love. And how strange in those moments all the fleeting ends of night and time returned without recall. Segments of half-forgotten songs, faces swept away on passing trains, first bloom of buds in spring, lonely and restless autumn and the rending of thunder.

She sat up suddenly and listened, her shadowed body inclined toward the windows. Her small firm breasts down slightly and the dark nipples like ripe grapes upon the vine.

"Do you hear the thunder?" she asked.

"Yes," I said.

"I'm glad it's thundering tonight," she said.

"The ghosts of Greek warriors are dancing," I said. "They have lit campfires on the sides of the mountains and are dancing for our love."

She came gently to rest across my body. Her cheek across my bare chest and the clean silken softness of her hair teasing my flesh.

"Will it always be like this?" she asked.

"I don't know," I said. "Can it ever be just like this again?"

She looked down my legs and her soft fingered hand with moist palms touched my navel and flowed on.

"He is sleeping now," she said softly. "He is weary and asleep like a child that has played too hard."

The wonder that she should find pleasure in touching my flesh as I found pleasure in touching hers. The wonder of her lithe and naked body in my arms beneath the darkness of approaching storm.

She moved her head and twisted her body across my arms and came beside me with her head on my pillow. She closed her eyes and her lips quivered in soft and even breath.

"Where are they now?" she said and her voice seemed to come from far away. "Where are all the men and women who danced to our joy? Where is the earth I have known, and the years I have been alone?"

She drew closer and her leg ran the length of my own with her toes against my ankle. Our bodies touched and little beads of our sweat ran together. The thunder sounded louder, coming closer, and the shades rapped more restlessly at the windows.

Back in the hall the empty glasses of wine would litter the tables along the wall. The grease from the cold lamb would have hardened upon the plates. On the worn tablecloths the new wine stains would glisten like blood. Most of the celebrants would be gone, but one of the musicians had been hired till three and he probably still played, drink-heavy on the platform, slapping the protesting strings of his lyre.

A few would still dance, a few would still watch. A little too full of wine and lamb they would circle the beaten floor dropping out finally one by one, lingering for a moment beside the tables and then gathering their coats and walking the dim corridor down the stairs and into the street.

The lyre would be put away and the last of the men and women would stand uncertainly in the empty hall that felt cold without the music and suddenly dark with pressing shadows as the janitor began to snap off the lights.

The last ones would move, keeping a few feet before the closing lights. The door to the street opening and closing for the last time. The deserted tables with the stained cloths would spring squarely into darkness.

Where were they now? All the men and women who danced to our union and left the hall into dark night.

Where were Simonakis and Gerontis and Falcounis and all the other old men of Hellas who had ancient fires to keep them warm? Old men who lived secure in blooded memory of a world that knew honor and dignity and strength.

Where was Mike, my tall and straight brother, and his Sheila who lost her first child? Would they listen tonight to thunder, free of bitterness and blood, and think of us and seed again?

Where was Father Kontoyannis who could no longer bear to weep and smile from one face? Who waited as Abraham and Job had waited for word of the divinity of their God.

Where was my father?

Was he sitting in the big dark house alone, listening to thunder, thinking of the past? For in the hour of my marriage he must have become aware of the waning of his years. He must know now, in the moment of my fulfillment, the vulnerableness of his flesh and the blindness that would come to his eyes and the cold earth that would hold the rocks that were his arms.

But I would not cry for him. In the shadowed room with the thunder rising and my wife asleep in my arms I would cry once more for the past that was gone, for the warm loved past that could never be regained, but I would not cry for him.

For in that moment of swelling thunder and nourished love I understood how he could not bear that the heroes were gone. That Ajax and Achilles and Odysseus no longer hurled lances and howled their great war cries before the ramparts of Troy. He could not suffer to live quietly in our time of dwarfs. For him the fury and fire of the mills, the blazing furnaces, the flashing rolls were once again the battlegrounds of Troy and Thermopylae and Salamis. He was of a race of mighty men belonging to another age. His spirit as much flame as the spirits of Hector and Achilles and Odysseus and all the valiant men who lived like lions on this dark and unfathomable earth.

I think I fell asleep just as the rain began.